The Book of Dead Birds

The Book of
Dead Birds

[A NOVEL]

Gayle Brandeis

HarperCollins*Publishers*

HarperCollins books may be purchased for educational, business, or sales promotional use. For information, please write: Special Markets Department, HarperCollins Publishers Inc., 10 East 53rd Street, New York, NY 10022.

A continuation of this copyright appears on page 243.

FIRST EDITION

Designed by Nancy Singer Olaguera

Printed on acid-free paper

Library of Congress Cataloging-in-Publication Data

Brandeis, Gayle.
    The book of dead birds : a novel / Gayle Brandeis.—1st ed.
        p. cm.
    ISBN 0-06-052803-6
    1. Women conservationists—Fiction. 2. Birds—Effect of water pollution on—Fiction. 3. Korean American women—Fiction. 4. Mothers and daughters—Fiction. 5. Racially mixed people—Fiction. 6. Salton Sea (Calif.)—Fiction. 7. San Diego (Calif.)—Fiction. I. Title.

PS3602.R345 B66 2003

813'.6—dc21

2002032894

03 04 05 06 07 ❖/RRD   10 9 8 7 6 5 4 3 2 1

for Matt

I had a dove and the sweet dove died;
  And I have thought it died of grieving.
O, what could it grieve for? Its feet were tied,
  With a silken thread of my own hand's weaving.

—JOHN KEATS

If you go back far enough in my family tree there are birds.

—SUSAN MITCHELL

The Book of Dead Birds

I remember the first time I flew.

I was four years old. My mother decided to take me to Balboa Park for the afternoon. I watched the back of her short-sleeved blouse as we crossed the parking lot to the playground; the sky-blue fabric tightened, then loosened, tightened, then loosened, across her shoulder blades, pointy as chicken wings. I tried to catch up, but my mother was too fast. Even then, I knew she didn't like to be seen with me in public. I knew it was because of my skin—so much darker than my mother's, dark like the treats she made out of dates that morning, the ones that stuck between my teeth, filling my mouth with a prickly sweetness.

We didn't go to the park very often, but this day was special— New Year's Eve, 1975. Not December 31, when midnight bullets flew through our San Diego neighborhood and we crouched together in the closet; this was a few weeks later—the lunar New Year, the Korean New Year, the day when girls stand up on seesaws and swings.

At four, I was already as tall as my mother's ribs. I broke into a run and tugged at my mother's shirt, pulling it out of the elastic waistband of her lime-green pants. She shook herself loose and kept walking. I could see the scar on her lower back as her shirt flapped up—a crescent moon, beaded with pale tooth marks. I reached to swipe a finger over it, but she walked even faster.

She let me catch up to her when we reached the grass. Without looking at me, she looped two fingers around my wrist and guided me over to the swings. She lifted me by the armpits with a grunt and deposited me, standing, on a swing strap. I clutched the chain while she moved the swing lightly back and forth, but I couldn't keep my balance. I wobbled, then tumbled into her arms.

She glanced around to make sure no one was watching, then shifted me onto her hip and lurched over to the seesaw. With her foot, she tilted one end of the peeling yellow plank to the ground; I grabbed on to her sleeves.

"No, Omma!" I yelled, as she set me, standing, on the edge.

"You stay here." She twisted herself away from my grip.

"Omma!" I jumped off the seesaw. The plank rose into the air. She pushed it down again and set me back on.

"You stay now." Her voice was firm.

I couldn't breathe as I watched my mother walk to the other side of the playground. I wanted to step off the seesaw but my feet felt bolted to the plank. When she finally stopped and turned around, my throat filled with air.

"Omma!" I spread out my arms. She began to run toward me.

I had never seen my mother run before. She was fast. I watched her cheeks jiggle and her mouth sway loose and her small breasts swing around as she came closer. Then she jumped. She jumped as if there were a trampoline in the grass. She shot up so high, I worried she might get tangled in the jacaranda branches above. There was a determination in her eyes that scared me. It scared her, too. I could see her hesitate as she began to fall. She pedaled her feet backward like a cartoon character who realized he had just walked off a cliff, but she landed on the seesaw anyway, a crumpling blur of limbs.

That's when I flew.

I flew straight over my mother's head, flew like a bullet across the playground. I felt as if I wouldn't ever stop, as if I would keep on flying, past the park, past the zoo and the stores and the ocean. I felt as if I would be a flying girl forever. Then a eucalyptus tree zoomed toward my face. My mother tackled me to the ground just as I was about to hit the molting trunk.

Neither of us spoke on the car ride home. We barely even breathed—it felt as if one loud exhale would make some invisible seesaw between us lose its precarious balance. As soon as we got into the apartment, I stumbled off to bed. I felt my end of the ghost board clatter to the ground, felt my mother float untethered behind me as I drifted into a deep, dark nap.

When I woke, my whole head throbbed. My forehead had banged into the dirt pretty hard when we fell. In the gray light of dusk, I could see my mother sitting by the window, rocking a bit, as if she had to go to the bathroom.

"Omma." My voice was a puff of air.

My mother turned toward me, then crept up to the bed. Something about her looked different, scary. Her eyebrows, I realized, were completely white. She had put some kind of powder on them; flecks of it dusted her eyelashes, her cheeks, her collar. After I walked to the bathroom, I was startled to find my own eyebrows white, as well. They looked strange on my much darker face, like a powdered sugar decoration, frosting on a gingerbread cookie. A scrape ran across my forehead, an oblong abrasion, speckled pink and red. I touched a finger to it; pain shot behind my eyes. I began to feel dizzy. My mother grabbed me by the arms and led me back to bed.

"If you take nap at New Year," she told me as she tucked me under the covers, "the story says your eyebrow turn white. Is joking to put on flour if you fall asleep."

My mother didn't look happy to me, not like someone telling a joke. "Did you fall asleep, Omma?" I asked.

She shook her head. A tear carved a streak through the light dusting of flour on her face.

I pressed a finger against the damp trail, then stuck my finger in my mouth. It tasted like paste, like salt.

She was silent for a moment before she whispered, "I want to show you."

"Show me what?"

"I want you can see . . ."

Specks of flour drifted past my eyelashes. My mother smoothed the pilly bedspread over my thighs.

"Long time ago," she said, "girls and women live in walls."

"We live in walls." I rubbed at my eyes. "If we didn't live in walls, we'd live in the sky."

"Stone walls," she said. "A big fence, all around the yard. Girls, women, not able to go to the world."

"That's silly." I wanted to go back to sleep. My whole skull throbbed.

"New Year's different."

"They could go outside?" I could still see my mother running toward me as if in slow motion, her whole body rippling like gelatin. I could still see my mother jump. My stomach pitched with the sudden rush of flight.

"They had the *noldwigi*. Long wood on a bag of rice straw. A seesaw."

"So?"

"So they see."

"Omma." I winced. My forehead felt like it would crack open if I tried to think too hard.

"The girls, they jump on the *noldwigi,* they jump the other one up, let her see over the wall. Just a little look. Once a year, over the stone. They show each other."

She sank to her knees.

I turned my pounding head to the window. A pigeon landed on the ledge outside. Its throat shimmered with the sunset.

M y name is Ava Sing Lo.

I am a bird killer. The killer of my mother's birds. An accidental killer, but a killer nonetheless.

Someday I'll probably end up like Prometheus, chained to a rock, birds pecking away at my liver. Appropriate karma. Birds should peck at all my vital organs. I should be tarred with bird droppings and copiously feathered. I should be forced to swallow a whole sack of birdseed dry.

My mother named me Ava because she liked how the English letters looked—the big *A* a beak pointed upward, the *v* a sharp slash of wings, the small *a* round and flat as a parrot's eye. She chose the name even before she knew it had anything to do with birds—the letters spoke to her with their own hollow bones. Her family name was Song, but she chose Sing for us because—and this may be more my interpretation than hers—it sounded more active, like something that is happening, something alive in the throat, not something that has already been written down, sung a million times. I'm afraid I haven't lived up to that part of my name yet.

The "Lo," which I know I've lived up to (or, I should say, lived *down* to) comes from my mother's mishearing of the song "Swing Low, Sweet Chariot." She had seen an American movie where a man in prison sang that song, and she thought he was saying "*sing low*," his voice was so low, so gravelly and dark. That's how she felt twenty-five years ago, she's told me—low and gravelly and dark right after I was born. That's how I still make her feel, it seems, again and again and again, awkward as the "l" sound in her mouth.

*   *   *

Kane is my most recent victim. Psiticin Kane, who I named after I discovered the scientific name for parrots. Kane of the red tail feathers. Kane of the stunning bilingual vocabulary. Kane of the lemon pulp eyes. Kane, the African gray my mother thought would be her companion the rest of her life.

My intentions, as usual, were good. My mother was on a Las Vegas bus tour, and I arranged to have the carpet cleaned. She grew up on smooth stone floors and the seed-studded carpet grated on her nerves; I thought she would be thrilled when she came home and found soft clean shag beneath her feet. How was I to know parrots are so sensitive to cleaning products? I thought I had taken precautions—I had covered Kane's cage with a towel before the carpet cleaners came. He was nervous around new people and skittish about strange sounds. I always covered his cage before I pulled out my *chang'go.* I thought I had done enough.

When I got back home and took off my shoes to walk across the slightly damp carpet, I could tell something was wrong. Kane's normal greeting of *"Annyong hashimnikka?"—"Are you at peace?"*— was conspicuously absent.

"Animal crackers in my soup," I sang off-key. Unlike my mother, I am not much of a singer.

I had bought a package of animal crackers for Kane, his favorite treat. He liked to walk around the cage with the string of the circus-train box dangling from his beak, like a handbag.

"Monkeys and rabbits loop de loop," I continued.

Usually at this point, Kane joined in with "Gosh oh gee but I have fun . . . ," but there was no Shirley Temple response from under the terry cloth. I hoped it was because he wasn't used to singing with me—my mother was the one who usually shared this duet—but I had a sinking suspicion this wasn't the case.

I softly added the next part, despite Kane's silence: "Swallow-ing animals one by one."

I took a deep breath, then pulled the towel from the cage. Kane lay on the spattered newspaper. His pale yellow eyes were glazed. He trembled as if he had just taken a dip in freezing water.

The box of animal crackers fell out of my hand and burst open on the ground. I opened the cage, pulled Kane out, wrapped him in the towel, and ran downstairs without putting my shoes back on.

"Has your bird recently been exposed to any chemical or caus-tic fumes?" Dr. Miller asked me as he listened to Kane's chest.

"I just had the carpet cleaned." I watched his freckled hands.

"Bird's lungs are very sensitive." The vet moved his stetho-scope. A strand of his curly orange hair fell on Kane's belly. I brushed it away. "You should never expose them to industrial cleaning products."

I should have known Kane had weak lungs. He had come down with psittacosis a couple of years before. My mother came down with it, too, and I had to take a week off from San Diego State, walking between sick mother and sick bird, administering droppersful of antibiotics and ginseng and seaweed soup.

"We're going to have to do an aspiration," Dr. Miller told me. "It would be best if you wait outside."

I bounced my heels up and down as I sat in the small waiting room. A pug drooled on my shins, but I couldn't find the energy to shoo him away. Dr. Miller walked through the swinging doors, and a small surge of hope rose inside my chest.

"I'm afraid we weren't able to save your bird," he said. "We did everything we possibly could. The damage was just too extensive."

All I could do was nod. My heart clattered against the bottom of my rib cage like a fallen plate.

"There was a last word." The vet's voice brightened a bit. "I don't know if it was a word—it was actually more of a sound. Something like hee hee hammy something . . ."

My whole body suddenly turned cold. "I don't understand."

"I'm afraid I don't either," he said. "I thought it might be gibberish, but . . ."

"*Ihae mot hamnida* is probably what he said. It means 'I don't understand' in Korean." My voice cracked like it does when I sing.

Dr. Miller looked at me strangely—trying, I'm sure, to figure out why a dark-skinned, barefoot woman like myself would know Korean.

"Kane used to say it a lot." A tear slid into my mouth. "It was like his little joke."

Do I have it on tape? I wondered. I sometimes recorded my mother's birds' voices to use as MIDI samples. I hoped I had something left of Kane for my mother to press to her ear.

The vet cleared his throat.

"I'm sorry for your loss." He briefly touched my shoulder. "I'll have the receptionist bring the body out shortly."

I watched him walk back into the clinic with a flap of white coattails, flounce of orange hair. I thought of the strand of his hair that fell on Kane's belly, brassy against the pale gray, as shocking a contrast as Kane's red tail feathers had been. My mother loved those feathers. She had saved the brown baby ones in a Ziploc bag and was so excited when the red ones came in, even though she usually associates red with the Korean Book of Death and never wears it herself or writes with a red pen.

The receptionist brought Kane out in a white paper bag, my name scrawled across it in thick black marker. One red feather poked past the crinkly paper lip. The immensity of what I had done suddenly bowled me over.

Oh, Omma. I closed my eyes. *Oh, Omma, I am so, so sorry.*

When I got home, my mother was picking pieces of animal cracker off the floor.

"The carpet wet," she said.

"I had it cleaned." I held Kane's bag behind my back.

"Smells." My mother pinched her nose, fanned her other hand in front of her.

We stood together in silence. The empty cage in the middle of the room spoke louder than either one of us could. My mother cocked an eyebrow up at me and I handed her the bag. She looked inside, nodded, and walked to her room.

"Omma." I stood at the door, but my mother didn't answer.

I knew what my mother would do. She would add Kane to her Book of Dead Birds. She would tape a feather onto a yellowed scrapbook page, write her reminiscences, paste in a photograph. She would press the cracked maroon leather cover to her chest and wail. She would yell that I was as bad as the army, storming in, killing every living thing in sight.

I knew what I would do, too. I would listen outside my mother's door. I would feel wave upon guilty wave of nausea. I would apologize until my jaws ached. I would search through my MIDI files for the bird's voice. I would—despite my most diligent efforts—most likely kill again.

Omma, I don't know if you'll ever read this, my own under-the-bed book. (Funny, isn't it? Should I paste in a bit of your hair? A nail clipping?) Everything you sing, I remember, I write down—

frantic notes and scribbles I hope I can flesh out on these pages, even if it scorches my own flesh in the process, even if the words have to claw their way out. I don't know if I'm getting it right—I know you think I don't get anything right—but this is what I've gleaned so far. Omma, if I can't save your birds, maybe I can save a little bit of your story.

Hye-yang wasn't sure she could hold her breath much longer. She watched her mother and grandmother swim five feet deeper underwater, scooping sea urchins off craggy volcanic rock. Their hair streamed around their faces as they turned to place the creatures into rope baskets strapped to their backs. Hye-yang swam toward them, bubbles escaping from her mouth. Just as she reached for an abalone shell, a sharp pain shot through her ribs. She pushed herself toward the surface, leaving her mother and grandmother behind.

Hye-yang broke through the skin of the water, gasping. Three white pelicans flew past her, eyeing her basket. As they swooped down a few feet away, Hye-yang noticed a man sitting on a rock on the shore, silhouetted against the gray sky.

Uneasy, Hye-yang swam toward him.

"You are not allowed here," she said to the man as she walked out of the water. It was unlawful for men to watch the women divers on Cheju-do. Hye-yang, at eighteen, had just started to dive.

"I heard you singing, before, before you went underwater." The man stood up on the rock. He wore a dark, shiny blue suit and tie, not the traditional clothes worn on Cheju-do. His hair was slicked back. A cigarette dangled from one hand. "You have a beautiful voice."

Hye-yang crossed her arms over her chest. She knew the loose white diving garment turned see-through when wet. She hadn't been singing; she had been letting the air out of her lungs, sending out an *eieieieieieie* that filled the whole cove before she dove underwater.

"I would like to offer you a job," he said. "Singing. At a night-club, on the mainland. Our girls do very well."

"I am a diver, not a singer." Hye-yang set her rope basket onto the rocky ground.

"You could be very famous." The man threw down his cigarette and jumped off the rock. He walked up to her and pulled a pink card from his inner jacket pocket.

Hye-yang did not reach for it.

The man stepped even closer. He slid the card beneath Hye-yang's wet collar, then reached his hand deeper. Hye-yang froze as his fingers grazed her nipple.

"You will call me." He smiled as he drew his hand back out of her clothes, but his eyes were cold.

Hye-yang felt the card, plastered to her skin, start to slide down her left breast. She began to shiver uncontrollably, but she couldn't move. She watched the man light another cigarette and walk away.

Hye-yang's mother and grandmother soon came up behind her. She could hear the water drip off their bodies, a light patter against the ground.

"Hye-yang," her mother said sharply as she dropped her heavy bag. "Was a man talking to you?"

"I told him he wasn't supposed to be here," Hye-yang said.

Hye-yang's grandmother gestured to the card glowing through Hye-yang's clothes. She reached in and pulled it out.

"What is this?"

"He told me I could be a singer."

"Well, you're not much of a diver." Hye-yang's mother laughed gruffly. She picked up Hye-yang's rope bag and shook the small number of abalone shells out onto the rough dark sand.

Hye-yang's grandmother threw the card back at her. She and Hye-yang's mother walked away, dragging their rope bags full of hard and spiny animals. Hye-yang could hear them saying something about more and more shame.

Hye-yang crumpled to the ground, tears spilling down her face. She had brought shame to her family's house even before she was born. In utero, she was promised as a bride to a neighbor's two-month-old son, but a week and a half before she was born, the boy succumbed to crib death. Hye-yang came into the world a widow, a fallen woman. No man would ever want to marry her, her mother was always quick to mention.

Hye-yang scooped the abalone shells back into the bag. Still shivering, she made her way back home, past the barley fields and acres of yellow rapeseed flowers, the pink card curled soggy in her hand.

A spray of gulls flew overhead, crying into the wind. Hye-yang walked faster. Tall *harubang,* grandfathers carved from volcanic rock, lined the dirt path. Despite their goofy faces, the stones looked menacing to Hye-yang, dark and foreboding against the gathering storm. The abalone shells clacked together in her rope basket in time with her steps.

Hye-yang looked at the pink business card. It was written in English, except for one Korean phrase that meant "we hire entertainment ladies." Her face smarted when she remembered the man's hand in her clothes. No man had ever touched her skin before, not even her hands. Her father may have held her, but he died when Hye-yang was three, and she couldn't remember anything about him.

Hye-yang turned the bend and her family's small stone house came into view, its thatched roof battened down with ropes and rocks. One pole was gone from the gate, a sign that her mother and grandmother were out, but not far. Hye-yang took down the other two poles and went inside. She peeled off her wet diving clothes and stood shivering before the kitchen fire as she looked at the business card again. If only the man had not touched her, Hye-yang would call. Maybe she should call anyway, she thought, eyeing the strange English letters. Hye-yang knew she was not helping her family as a diver. She was nothing but an embarrassment. If she went to the mainland and got a job, she could send money home, more than she could ever earn with her small catch of abalone. Plus, she loved to sing. When Hye-yang sang at the Snow Blossom Festival a few months before, her first time in front of an audience, she felt like her heart would soar right out of her skin.

Hye-yang put on some dry clothes. She brushed out her salty hair and thought about the phone at the farmer's coop kiosk, the closest one to her family's house. Hye-yang pulled on her jacket and grabbed a pouch of coins. Then she noticed an envelope on the floor, addressed to her, already opened, its contents jutting out.

Hye-yang recognized the handwriting immediately. The letter was from Hye-yang's friend Sun, who left Cheju-do four months before to work at the Korean Folk Village in Suwon. Hye-yang wanted to go with her, but her mother refused, saying she needed to stay and learn to dive.

There is still lots of work available here, Sun wrote, on paper thin as onion skin. Sun played a bride each weekend in a traditional wedding ceremony put on for tourists. During the week, she demonstrated women's seesaw. *Come visit me,* she pleaded. *I need a friend from the island. My best friend.*

Hye-yang missed Sun terribly. She missed their cave, the dark craggy cave they found together behind a waterfall, the one that led to strange tunnels and cold little pockets of space. They often took candles and red bean buns and explored the passages, bumping into each other in the dark, giggling with the fear and thrill of it. After Sun left, Hye-yang passed the mouth of the cave almost every day, but she couldn't bring herself to go inside of it alone.

If she were to leave the island, it would make sense to go to her friend, not to some nightclub in Kunsan where she didn't know anyone but a man with a shiny suit and rough hands. Hye-yang tossed the business card into the fire beneath the pot of rice. The soggy paper sputtered for a while, sizzling and twitching, before it collapsed into flames, sending black tongues of smoke up the sides of the pot.

Hye-yang's mother came through the door, waving her hand at the smoke that began to fill the room.

"You want to go?" she asked Hye-yang sharply, gesturing to the letter unfolded on Hye-yang's lap.

Hye-yang nodded her head. Across the room, her mother slowly disappeared into the swirling gray smoke.

"You go, then." Her mother's voice cut through the haze. "But don't you come flying back here. Don't even think you can come flying on back."

Red Lored Amazon (Name: Pippy)

Ava, daughter, 11. Kill bird with candy.
He sit on shoulder when she do homework,
give him MM out her hand. Every day
she give him some. One day he fall
back off shoulder, hard stone to the floor.
I don't know candy poison for bird.
Ava, she know?

[yellow-shelled chocolate crushed under tape]

[small red feather]

10/16/82
Helen Sing Lo's Book of Dead Birds

My mother works in bent silhouette, framed by the bright window across the room.

I rustle the newspaper, yesterday's, to try to get her attention. "Omma," I ask her, "where's Estonia?"

"Estonia Hotel downtown," she says, her voice muffled by her surgical mask. Between this and the sudden whir of the dentist's drill, I can barely hear her.

"The *country*, Omma." I flinch at the reminder of her knowledge of downtown hotels and glance again at the blurb in the *San Diego Union Tribune,* the one I've been saving for her. "Do you know where the country Estonia is? The article says it's Baltic, but I'm not really sure what that means. I think it's near Russia."

My mother grunts and presses a magnifying glass against her goggles. She stares intently at the scrollwork she's just drilled into an empty ostrich eggshell, the one she's turning into a music box. Her eggshell change purses, night lights, ships in bottles, picture frames sell at a small circuit of local craft fairs and gift shops.

"I have something for your book," I tell her. My mother's back slowly unhunches itself.

"Listen to this." I lift the paper. "'Thousands of swans are in danger of dying along the Baltic coast in Estonia as one of the harshest winters in years has frozen the shallow waters where they feed. Hundreds of swans have already starved to death. The remaining 5,000 are in danger of dying if, as forecast, the waters stay locked in ice for many weeks to come.'"

It sounds like my mother is saying something, but when I look up, her mask is still, collapsed against her lips. A wispy glow emanates from her backlit head, through the slim gaps in her teased-up hair. I am momentarily stunned by its corona. My own hair, cropped close to my skull, feels like a sudden, dense weight. No light could ever pass through it.

"They're trying to help, Omma. Here." I clear my throat and start to read again. "'In an effort to save the swans, rescue teams have smashed holes through some sections of the ice, frozen nearly two feet thick along the coast. A public appeal has also been made for people to feed bits of bread and potatoes to hungry swans languishing near the shore.'"

"Do you think swans would like *Oh-Jing-Uh Bok-Um?*" I try to joke a bit. "Birds eat squid, don't they? It's too bad we don't live closer by. Maybe we could ship it there."

My mother looks out the window. Her shoulders start to rise to her ears.

"The pepper paste might be a bit much for them . . ." I bite my lip and walk toward my mother, but she quickly flips her goggles back down, turns the drill back on, and starts to carve again.

I wave my hand in front of my face to keep the eggshell dust out of my nose and mouth, then trudge off to my room. The room I moved back into after I finished my masters in communications at San Diego State and couldn't get enough steady work as a sound engineer to pay my own rent. The room I'm not sure I'll ever quite escape from.

The fact that I have a degree—two degrees—in communications is a bit of a joke. I spent most of my time at school behind a sound-board with headphones clamped over my ears. I didn't have to communicate much with anyone. I'm just grateful for my drum. Without it, I don't think I could communicate with my mother at all.

The article about the Estonia swans will end up in my mother's scrapbook by the end of the day, I'm sure of it. I flop down on my bed and grab a lump of candied ginger from the bag on the nightstand. My mouth fills with its bright, soapy flavor. I can imagine flying off to Estonia, wherever it is, with bushels of bread and potatoes and covered dishes of spicy squid. I can imagine standing at the frozen shoreline, tossing food everywhere, crumbs disappearing like light down one cygnet throat after another. I can imagine hefting swans under each arm, carrying them back to my tiny hotel room that smells of borscht and wet wool.

I can almost feel the birds' solid weight strain against my biceps as I work a fibrous strand of ginger between my teeth. I can see myself folding the swans into dog carriers for the long flight back to San Diego. I can see myself filling my mother's bathtub with the birds, the living, unharmed birds, their long necks swooping against the shower curtain, their beaks cool and smooth as plastic against my palm.

I swallow the broken threads of ginger and listen to my mother's drill buzz like a mosquito in the next room. Kane's recorded voice occasionally rises above the hum—*I don't understand. I don't understand. Are you at peace?*

Ava, daughter, age 6.
Go to park together.
No seesaw,
pond full of birds.
Bring bread from home
to feed in pieces.
Ava walk up to goose—
soft brown body,
black head, black neck,
stripe of white under chin.
She gives bread.
Too big piece, maybe?
Ava lift up hands,
bird fall down,
stick pink tongue
from black beak.
Look like person tongue,
so pink. Didn't know bird
could have pink tongue.

—5/23/73

Against my better judgment, I buy my mother a zebra finch, scrabbling madly inside a Chinese take-out container, from a man on a blanket outside the Tae Kwon Do studio. My mother names him Yukam, "Regret." She keeps him in a cage by her bed and bars me from her room.

I wake up around 3:00 A.M. to the sound of my mother's singing. It is the *pansori*, of course. I grab my *chang'go* and sleepily carry it out into the dark living room. My mother is sitting there on the floor, Yukam settled squarely on top of her head.

My mother once told me that *pansori* singers train by standing underneath a waterfall and singing until their voices cut through the rush of water. They practice until they spit up enough blood from their throats to fill three large jugs. Listening to her voice, it's easy to believe this.

I sit cross-legged and begin to thrum at the hourglass-shaped drum in response to my mother's song. *Pansori* songs can go on for hours; my mother always weaves her own words in with the traditional lyrics. Often, she forgoes the traditional lyrics entirely. Bits of her life stream out of her, in English, in Korean, of which I unfortunately have very limited knowledge. She periodically stands up, whips her folded fan around, lifts her arms in sweeping gestures, then she sits back down, her voice a touch quieter, her face still blazing with her story. I talk with my mother through the drum—soft, sympathetic, thrums at times, angry thumps at others. The song doesn't stop until the room is tinged with the first wash of morning light. I go back to my room and write down as much as I can remember.

Hye-yang told her mother and grandmother it was her bleeding time, so she would be excused from diving for the day. She imagined the women were reaching for sea urchins as she stuffed her clothes into a bag, looped her archery bow over her shoulder, and walked through the open gate without replacing the three wooden poles behind her.

As she hiked along a rocky ridge above the ocean, Hye-yang thought she could see figures in white garments traveling parallel to her under the water. She wondered if her mother and grandmother were following her, echoing her steps with their ghostly glide. Hye-yang sped up her pace, hoping to lose them, when a gull dove through what she had thought was her mother's head. Hye-yang's feet froze beneath her until the bird came back up, a fish thrashing in its beak. The billowy image in the water shuddered, then righted itself again, and she realized it was only the reflection of some clouds.

When she got to the ferry docks, Hye-yang half expected to find her mother and grandmother, dripping and angry, waiting for her, but aside from the ticket taker and some uniformed workers, only a few honeymoon couples milled around by the boat. Hye-yang paid her fare, then climbed aboard the ferry.

She rested her bow against a bench and leaned her stomach against the railing at the front of the boat. The water stretched out forever in front of her, vast and blue and brilliant. A surge of excitement, laced with fear, rushed through her body as the boat lurched, then began to pull away from the dock. Hye-yang had never left the island's orbit before. She waved at some pelicans as they flew by, their wings fully open, white feathers glinting in the sun.

The ferry arrived in Pusan eight hours later, at dusk. Hye-yang was stunned by the sight of the large city, already lit up for night. As she walked down the ramp off the boat, Hye-yang's sea legs buckled beneath her; she had to brace herself with the tip of her bow as she walked toward the terminal.

Inside, Hye-yang bought a bowl of buckwheat noodles in sweet radish sauce, and a cup of walnut tea. Hungry as she was, she found it hard to eat, overwhelmed by the number of people around her, all moving so fast. Human voices filled the space like bird chatter. The air smelled strongly of smoke and armpits and fish. Every time someone walked by, it stirred up a new layer of scent. Hye-yang hugged her bow to her body to keep it from getting smashed.

She slurped up a few noodles, then pushed her way through the crowd until she found the bus with a SUWON placard hanging above it. She squeezed herself, her bag, and her bow on board and fell into the last available seat.

The bus smelled like the terminal, but even more intense. Hye-yang tried to get comfortable in her narrow seat, her bow tipped against her chest and shoulder, but she wasn't quite successful. An elderly woman sat next to her, sound asleep. The scent of squid drifted from her open mouth.

Hye-yang gaped out the window at the tall buildings as the bus pulled away from the station and made its way slowly through a maze of streets, sound and smoke pouring through the scattered open windows.

Just a few minutes into the ride, the bus got snagged in a traffic jam. Hye-yang noticed a crowd of men milling on the street outside, standing in front of windows, going in and out of buildings; men in Western business suits, mostly, but a few wearing old-fashioned *chogori.* The street was lined with storefronts featuring huge window-panes, all of them glowing inside with a harsh pink light. In every window sat at least one woman wearing an elaborate *hanbok* and makeup, posed in a little traditional tableau.

The old woman next to Hye-yang stirred.

"Ahhh, Wanwol-dong," she sleepily muttered to Hye-yang.

"Excuse me?" Hye-yang asked.

"This area—its name is Wanwol-dong," the woman yawned.

"What are the women doing in those windows?" Hye-yang asked.

"You don't know?" The woman looked at Hye-yang, surprised.

"Is it some sort of cultural display?" Hye-yang asked, thinking the street might be some urbanized version of the Folk Village she was traveling to in Suwon.

The woman snorted.

"Are they selling those *hanbok*s?" Hye-yang looked at the colorful costumes, the large sleeves trailing to the ground.

"They're selling what's in those *hanbok*s, daughter," the woman said matter-of-factly before she closed her eyes again.

Hye-yang stared for a second at the white whiskers sprouting on the woman's upper lip before she looked back out the window, shocked.

Traffic began to move again. Hye-yang tried to see the faces of the women as the bus drove down the street, but their features smeared together in the pink glare of the endless storefronts.

Hye-yang's lids still pulsed with colored light when she closed her eyes. The business card the man had given her at the beach flashed into her mind. It had left a pink stain on her breast, like a bright little window to her heart. She wasn't able to wash it off for days. Hye-yang opened her eyes again and grimaced as her seat-mate made a few more wet smacking sounds. As the bus picked up speed, she turned her head and watched the pink haze recede into the background, garish as the sunset.

When I wake up a few hours later, my hand is still a bit numb. I flex and blow on my fingers to limber them up before I get out of bed and join my mother in the kitchen.

She is standing over a pot of *Hae-jang-guk,* "morning-after" soup. Her eyes are red and puffy. I figure it's from lack of sleep until I realize she is crying.

"Omma, are you okay?" I lightly touch her shoulder. "Did something happen to Yukam?" I feel overwhelmingly guilty, even though I know I've done nothing wrong.

My mother shakes her head. She spoons out a bowl of soup for herself and walks across the kitchen with it steaming in her hands.

"Omma?" I follow after her, but she goes into her room and closes the door.

I stand in front of the door for a moment before I return to the kitchen. I ladle up my own bowl of soup and bring it to the low coffee table in the dining area. The *Union-Tribune* is folded on my mother's cushion; I pick it up and shake it open. Two holes are cut out of the front section—one a small square, the other a long rectangle with a thin arm jutting out on top.

No longer hungry, I dump my bowl of soup into the sink. Three robins' eggs sit on a dishcloth by the basin, ready to have their insides blown out. I carefully move them, then the soup pot, into the refrigerator so that they won't spoil.

In the evening, my mother finally comes out. Her eyes are practically swollen shut, her skin blotchy.

"Omma, what can I do?" I ask from the kitchen. My head feels fuzzy, my hands sore. All day, I've been trying not to listen to the sobs coming from my mother's room. All day, I've been keeping myself busy, napping, practicing my tae kwon do *hyung*s, drumming a bit to keep my hand from cramping up. I set the pot of soup back on the stove to reheat it.

"No soup." Her voice is raspy. She grabs her purse and keys and heads for the door.

"Where are you going?"

"To drive."

"Do you want me to come with you? It's getting dark."

My mother shakes her head. She slips on a nylon windbreaker even though the air is still warm.

"Are you sure?"

She nods, not looking at me.

"Chosim haseyo," I tell her. "Be careful." Kane used to say it whenever he saw her leave the apartment.

She pauses for a moment.

"Don't go near Yukam," she warns before she closes the door behind her.

I stir the soup, but I'm no longer hungry. I put the foil back over the pot and turn off the burner.

If I want to see the new entries in her scrapbook, I'm going to have to be quick about it. Who knows how long she'll be gone?

The brassy doorknob to her room looks like it will give me an electric shock, but it feels cool against my hand, flimsy, almost too easy to turn. I open the door a crack. The bedroom is dark and smells of seaweed. I push the door a bit further and stick my head inside. Yukam's wing brushes my cheek as he flies out.

"No, Yukam!" I yell. "No no no! Come back!"

The bird flies in circles around the apartment, lighting briefly upon the curtains, the coffee table, the back of the sofa. He flies into the kitchen and bombs droppings onto the foil that covers the soup pot. I chase after him, looking up, arms outstretched. I trip over the cushions on the floor, hit my shins on the coffee table, bang my ribs into the kitchen counter. Yukam lands on a windowsill.

"No!" I yell when I see the window is open. I dive toward him.

Just as the bird is about to escape, I clap both hands over his small body. When I lift him to my chest, it feels like I'm holding my own wildly fluttering heart.

The sound of footsteps approaches the front door, then the jangle of keys. I race to my mother's room, throw Yukam inside, and shut the door. When my mother enters the apartment, I lean against the wall, attempting to look casual. I'm panting like crazy.

"I forget something." My mother looks at me suspiciously.

I nod, trying to catch my breath.

"What you have going on?" she asks.

"Nothing, Omma," I tell her. "I just thought I'd get some exercise. I was jogging in place . . ." I pantomime running.

She squints at me, then walks to the kitchen. I sag back against the wall, hoping she won't notice the droppings on the soup pot.

"You have my eggs?" Her voice rises.

"The robins' eggs?" I walk over to her. "I put them in the fridge to keep them fresh."

She lunges for the refrigerator. She pulls out the dish towel that cradles the three tiny blue eggs. Carefully, she puts each one on her tongue and closes her mouth.

"Omma, what are you doing?"

She glares at me, her mouth full.

"The air is so warm," I tell her. "I thought you'd want me to keep them fresh for you. I know you don't like blowing rotten eggs."

My mother opens her mouth. The three blue shells wobble precariously inside. She lifts them from her tongue and puts them into another dish towel, then tucks the small bundle under her shirt.

"I find the eggs on the ground," she says. "The nest fall down. I try to hatch, but you freeze to death!"

"Oh, Omma." My knees buckle. I sit down on the floor. "I thought you wanted to turn them into a necklace or something."

"I want to turn them into birds!" she yells.

I put my face in my hands.

The door slams behind my mother as she leaves the apartment again.

I sit on the floor a few minutes, my palms mashed against my eye sockets, a bright blizzard sparking behind my lids. When I open my eyes and stand up, the fierce speckles are still there, swarming the whole kitchen, dissolving everything for a moment into atoms, or dust. I wad up the soiled tinfoil from the soup pot, throw it away, and dump the rest of the soup down the sink. The broth scent wafts from the drain like bad breath.

I walk back to my mother's room, open the door without hesitation, and slip into the darkness, closing it behind me before Yukam can fly out.

The bird swoops past, stirring up the scent from my mother's half-eaten bowl of soup as I click on the light. I kneel down and pull the *Book of Dead Birds* out from under the bare mattress. I flip through the thick pages, turning my head so that I won't have to read about my murderous past. When my finger finds a page still a bit squishy with glue, I let myself look. Two articles, their shapes corresponding to the holes in the morning paper, cover the yellowed paper. The glue shines dully through the newsprint.

The first headline blares, "GI Not Charged in Death of Korean Prostitute." A woman was killed in the U.S. camptown of Osan, it says. A soda bottle had been jammed so far up her vagina, it perforated her uterus. The handle of an umbrella had torn open her rectum. Her neck had been broken, her face badly bruised. The U.S. Army chose to not press any charges against the GI responsible for the crime. Even though the people of Osan vehemently protested the inaction, the article suggests nothing further will be done.

No wonder my mother was so upset.

I set the book on the bed and stretch my arms out, shake them to shake the story out of my limbs. One of my hands flops against my mother's soup bowl. It wobbles precariously on the dresser, sends a fat wave of broth over the edge. I steady the bowl, then quickly grab some of my mother's crumpled tissues to mop up the spill. They wither and dissolve in the cold salty puddle. I use the edge of my shirt to clean up the rest, then pick up the bowl to wipe underneath it. A black-and-white photograph sits there, the edges and bottom lightly stained with soup. I carefully lift the picture and set it on the leg of my pants. The paper is a bit soggy, but the image itself is clear.

Two women stare up from my thigh. Their arms are looped around each other's waists, their smiles broad. An egret stands on one foot behind them, off to the left. Another bird's wing blurs over their heads. One woman, who I don't recognize, wears a traditional Korean wedding ensemble. The other is dressed in an old-fashioned-looking *hanbok,* a large archery bow tilted against her hip. I recognize the bow, but I barely recognize my mother. I've never seen a photograph of her smiling before. I've never seen her smile before, period—not like this. Usually she keeps her lips closed, straight, her upper lip puffed out a bit, as if stuffed with dental cotton. The smile in this picture is large and unguarded. It takes my breath away. I run a finger lightly over my mother's sodden face before I move the photo to the back of the scrapbook. Hopefully it will press dry.

A greenish square remains on my pants where the photo sat, matching the stain that spreads across the bottom of my shirt. I pull the seaweed-flecked cloth away from my body and begin to close the scrapbook, eager to change into some dry clothes, but then I remember I haven't read the other article yet. I twist the bottom of my shirt into a knot and spread the book back open.

"Poison Link Suspected in Bird Deaths," reads the next headline. The dateline is the Salton Sea, an inland lake eighty miles north of San Diego, in the middle of the desert. Over three thousand birds have died there in the last two weeks, 597 of them endangered California brown pelicans. I glance at the small map at the bottom of the article. The body of water is shaped like a lopsided *chang'go.*

The birds have been dying of botulism, the article reports. Officials believe the outbreak may stem from fish killed by pesticide misuse, since endosulfan had been illegally sprayed on private agricultural land south of the sea and had recently leached into the wildlife refuge. Thousands of fish showed up dead in the runoff ditches that drain into the sea; many sank to the bottom but were churned up by a fast, fierce thunderstorm, then cooked rancid in the returning desert sun. Contaminated maggots washed out from the rotting fish and were gobbled by pelicans, who started to show signs of sickness shortly after the storm. The surviving birds, the article states, are now being treated by volunteers.

Yukam lands on my lap. I close my hands around him and carry him to his cage.

"No more flying the coop for you, buster." I click the wire door shut.

"The surviving birds are now being treated by volunteers," I read again. I close the scrapbook, lift up a corner of my mother's mattress, and slide it back underneath.

Ava, daughter, give me book for birthday,
BIRDS OF AMERICA by John James Audubon.
Little flags stick out of book. "These are birds
that died," she tell me, "birds that are extinct
any more. Please note I do not kill any of them."
She run out of room, eat no cake.

I open book to flag at ivory-billed woodpecker:

When wounded and brought to the ground, the Ivory-
bill immediately makes for the nearest tree, and
ascends it with great rapidity and perseverance, until it
reaches the top branches, when it squats and hides,
generally with great effect. Whilst ascending, it moves
spirally round the tree, utters its loud pait, pait, pait, at
almost every hop, but becomes silent the moment it
reaches a place where it conceives itself secure. They
sometimes cling to the bark with their claws so firmly,
as to remain cramped to the spot for several hours after
death. When taken by the hand, which is rather a
hazardous undertaking, they strike with great violence,
and inflict very severe wounds with their bill as well as
claws, which are extremely sharp and strong. On such
occasions, this bird utters a mournful and very
piteous cry.

3/13/86

The sound of the drill wakes me in the middle of the night. All I can see when I walk into the living room are my mother's hands, carving in the dim pool of her gooseneck lamp. When I see a robin's egg under the drill, my heart drops. I flick on the ceiling light. My mother flinches.

Without looking up from her work, she points her arm back toward the kitchen counter. A shoebox sits there, a desk lamp bent over it. I walk closer and peer inside. Nestled in a mishmash of cotton balls and scarves lies another robin's egg.

"It's still alive?" I reach a finger hesitantly toward the tiny speckled shell.

My mother turns off the drill and pulls the top of her surgical mask down to her chin.

"Don't touch," she says sharply. "Two die already."

She lets the mask snap back up. The drill whines back to life.

I can't contain a smile. A living egg!

"Omma?" I walk over to her. "Omma? I want to talk to you about something."

She continues to work as if she can't hear me.

"I think I'm going to go to the Salton Sea," I tell her. "I want to help those pelicans, Omma, the ones that are sick. I think I can help them."

My mother's drill jerks to the side. The blue eggshell shatters. A few yolky fragments spray my soup-stained shirt.

"See what you made me to do," she scolds, but when she looks up at me, her eyes are filled with something other than anger.

I have this dream quite often. A large egg sits in the middle of the living room, shining like water. It shudders, then hops, then fills with a wild tapping, like the roll of a snare drum. A sharp elbow, a familiar-looking elbow, pierces the shell from the inside. It is so slick with blood and yolk, I can't tell whether it is my mother's or my own. It flaps around, then stills. I wonder if it will find the strength to break all the way through.

The morning sun is surprisingly hot; the air conditioner in my Sonata staves off only some of it as I run errands, picking up things I'll need for the trip—toothpaste, deodorant, tampons, blank tapes, adapter cable, a fresh bag of candied ginger. Sweat drizzles down the back of my neck. I know the desert heat will be even more intense; I feel parched at the thought of it, my mouth dry as the sheets of seaweed my mother keeps on top of the refrigerator. I park in front of Luk's Market so I can get something to drink before I head home.

The window on the door of the market is broken, covered by a black garbage bag and duct tape, but an OPEN sign is looped over the doorknob. I push the door lightly.

"Hello?" I step into the dim store. No one answers. The only sound comes from the coolers humming in the back. I work my way toward them. A blast of cold air hits my skin as I slide a glass door open. I close my eyes to feel it better and reach in blindly for the bottle of raspberry sparkling water I know is right in front of my face.

"What you doing here?"

I am startled by Mr. Luk's voice. The bottle slips out of my hand and shatters against the floor. Cool water bubbles up between the straps of my sandals.

"I'm sorry, Mr. Luk." I bend over to pick up the pieces. I've been to this market dozens of times, but he is never happy to see me.

"You break, you buy," he says.

A small woman I haven't seen before comes running through a door near the coolers. One of her eyebrows is missing, replaced by a long puckered scar. She stands behind her husband and stares at me like she thinks she knows who I am.

"That girl Korean," I hear her tell him.

"What?" Mr. Luk barks back at her. "Are you a crazy woman? She no Korean girl."

"She is from Helen!" the woman says. She looks straight at me. "You are from Helen?"

"Yes!" I tell her. "Helen—that's my mother—Helen Sing Lo . . ."

The woman whispers frantically to her husband.

"This store is closed!" he says sharply.

"There's an open sign on the door. I was thirsty . . ."

"You pay for the drink!"

"Of course." I rummage through my wallet. I pull out a five-dollar bill, thrust it at him, and walk out of the store.

The woman comes running after me with change.

"Keep it." I open the car door.

"Your mother Helen old friend of mine." The woman pushes the bills and coins into my palm. "I sorry for my husband. Bad things happen here sometime. He just scared; just scared man."

I slide into the car, lean my head back. "I'm sorry . . ." I close the door.

The woman taps on the window. I roll it down.

"Have you eaten rice yet?" the woman asks.

I shake my head.

"I work with your mother when you was little girl," the woman says in a low voice, and digs into her deep apron pocket.

"Is there any problem?" The husband's voice is wound tight as he steps through the door of the market.

"No, no problem here!" the woman calls out. Her eyebrow scar twitches a bit.

"Tell your mother to see me," she whispers. She throws a hand-ful of miniature Crunch bars onto my lap before she runs back to the market. Her husband ushers her brusquely back inside and rips the open sign from the door before he slams it shut.

I unwrap a Crunch bar, let my teeth pass through the deep brown chocolate, the pale crisped rice inside. Such an easy balance between these two flavors; such an uneasy balance in my own life—chocolate and rice battling it out, creating something different, something neither flavor can really claim. When I'm around other Korean people, even my mother—maybe especially my mother—I feel so black. When I'm around other black people, I feel so Korean. When I'm around anyone else, I just feel Other. The only time I really feel at home in my skin is when I'm slamming against the skin of my drum, but even then I know I'm doing it all wrong.

My sophomore year of college, a man, Dr. Park, came to my ethnomusicology class to give a talk on Korean music. When he got to the section on *pansori,* I made the mistake of telling the class I play the *pansori* with my mother. I usually never spoke up in class—the words just popped out of me. My professor was stunned; Dr. Park was even more stunned when I mentioned I use the *chang'go.*

"The *chang'go* isn't for *pansori.*" He shook his head at me from across the lecture hall. "You know that, right? The *puk* is the traditional *pansori* drum."

"I don't have a *puk,*" I stammered. I had no idea that I had been using the wrong drum. "My mother taught me on the *chang'go.*" I didn't mention she had stolen the *chang'go* from the massage parlor where she worked at the time. It had been used as an end table there, the deerskin cluttered with plastic bottles of oil.

"Come up here." His voice was somewhere between a cajole and a bark.

I walked to the front of the room, my face burning.

He pushed a shiny red *chang'go* against my stomach, a stick into my right hand. "Show me," he said.

I looped the strap of the drum over my shoulder and began to tap out a few rhythms. I usually drum in response to my mother's song; my hands felt awkward, stiff in the quiet classroom.

"No, no, no." He watched me closely. "You are supposed to inhale when you strike the *kungp'yon,* exhale when you strike the *yolp'yon.*"

My breath caught in my chest. "This is how my mother taught me," I told him.

"Your mother taught you wrong." He took the *chang'go* back.

I shift and the small Crunch bars fall onto the floor of my car. The candy in my mouth suddenly feels cloying, like sweet mucus. It catches in my throat as I try to swallow it down.

At home, after about five glasses of water, I tell my mother I met a woman she used to work with. She looks suddenly suspended, like she is balanced on a thin wire.

"What woman?"

"Her married name is probably Luk. She works at Luk's Market, near Washington. Short woman, only one eyebrow . . ."

My mother wrinkles her face for a moment before her eyes light up. "Anchee?"

"She didn't say."

She grabs her keys and purse and races out of the apartment.

When I go into my room, I catch a glimpse of myself in the mirror over my dresser. My mother's sad eyes—the same shape, just with more of a lid—stare back at me. Her high, broad cheekbones rise under my skin. Three gulls flap past the window behind me. Their doubles skim across the mirror.

I bow shakily to myself and assume the *Choom Be,* the tae kwon do ready stance. I look at my reflection, fists waist high, held tight next to my body, shoulders square, legs wide, feet planted on the carpet. I wonder what in the world I could possibly be ready for.

A chicken darted in front of Hye-yang's feet as she passed through the stone walls that bordered the Folk Village. She stumbled to avoid the bird and pitched forward. The tip of her bow clunked against the ground like a cane; her bag of clothes threatened to come undone, the strap biting deep into her shoulder. The chicken fluffed itself and scurried away.

Hye-yang remained bent over a moment to catch her breath, amazed by how easily a small bird could knock her over. She readjusted her belongings and headed toward a row of craftspeople who were practicing their arts in front of small farmer's huts.

While tourists watched, women spun silk from cocoons roiling in an iron pot; a man swirled his calligraphy brush over a scroll; blacksmiths bent over their anvils; grandmothers tied expert knots, teenagers pounded rice into flour. How strange, thought Hye-yang, that people pay to watch other people work. People pretending they weren't being watched. Hye-yang felt dizzy—so much movement, so much concentrated staring, all around her.

She felt even more disoriented when she noticed a small stone house up ahead, built to resemble a home from Cheju-do. It looked just like her family's house—the same thatched roof held down with ropes and stones, the same volcanic rock fence. It was as if the house had been ferried over from the island with her and dropped onto the village grounds. Hye-yang stood before it, heart knocking wildly; a woman stepped outside the house, wearing a white diver's outfit. Hye-yang almost expected to see her mother's face, but the woman was young, around her own age. Hye-yang closed her eyes and took a deep breath. The air smelled like honeycomb and dry grass, not seaweed and wet rocks. She finally realized how far she was from home. She wasn't sure whether the lightness that filled her head was freedom or fear.

A sudden burst of gong and drumbeat fractured the air. The steady stream of visitors turned and headed toward the music. Hye-yang let herself get carried along. As the crowd parted to let the musicians through, she noticed they were part of a wedding procession. A priest walked behind the *chang'go* player, holding a wooden goose on a small tray, two ribbons tied around its neck. The groom walked solemnly behind him. Hye-yang's heart lifted when she realized that her friend Sun, the weekend "bride," was probably inside the elaborately carved wooden box carried on the shoulders of four men who followed the groom.

The men set the box—a wooden bird perched on each corner— onto the ground. Two women attendants in pink *hanbok*s helped the bride out. Even though her head was bent traditionally down, her face hidden behind her sleeves as the attendants led her to the proper place, Sun's forehead, the back of her neck were unmistakable. Hye-yang would know them anywhere. She pushed through the crowd to the front as the two women lowered Sun to her knees. The priest placed the wooden goose by her feet, then bent to the north and bowed twice.

Sun's face was covered for most of the ceremony, even during the several times the ceremonial cup was brought to her lips. When she finally raised her face above her sleeves, Hye-yang could see small pink circles painted on her cheeks. Without realizing what she was doing, Hye-yang began to wave frantically. Sun, who had looked so radiantly solemn, glanced over.

"Hye-yang!" she cried, a smile bursting across her face. Hye-yang waved harder.

The priest bent down and whispered fiercely to Sun. She nodded and the ceremony resumed, but Hye-yang could see Sun's
shoulders quaking with laughter under her *hanbok.*

Hye-yang waited for Sun by the empty platform after the wedding was over. Sun came out soon in a plainer *hanbok,* the bright
circles rubbed off her cheeks, her hair loose.

"I can't believe you're here!" Sun cried. "Are you staying? I can
get you a job!"

"That's why I came," said Hye-yang.

"Come on." Sun grabbed Hye-yang's hand.

Before the day was out, Hye-yang was an employee of the Folk
Village, slated to sell cuttlefish at a stand the following morning,
slated to room with Sun in the village dormitory that night.

The two of them stayed up late, catching up on island life, village life, sharing smuggled bottles of OB beer. Around five in the
morning, unable to sleep, Sun pulled Hye-yang outside. They
hopped a couple of low stone fences and ended up in the area
where Sun performed seesaw demonstrations. The moon, full as a
grapefruit, bathed the field in a pale, pulpy light.

"How high can you go?" asked Hye-yang.

"I'll show you." Sun led her to the wooden plank. Hye-yang
stepped onto the end of it.

Hye-yang watched, a bit nervous, Sun walk pretty far away
before she turned, ran toward the seesaw, and jumped onto the
other end.

A giddy, weightless feeling opened in Hye-yang's chest. She
tilted her head back, spread her arms out wide, and let the night
embrace her whole body as she rose into the air. If she opened her
mouth, she thought, the moon would slide right in.

"What can you see?" Sun called up to her.

"I think I can see the whole world!" yelled Hye-yang, before she
hit the ground and toppled over on her side.

Sun ran over to her. "Are you okay?"

Hye-yang nodded her head and started to laugh. She yanked Sun's leg until she crashed down next to her.

"Let's do it again." Hye-yang grabbed Sun's face.

They ran back to the seesaw.

"What can you see?" they yelled, as they flung each other into the air as high as they could.

"I can see the governor's palace!"

"I can see Hollywood, California!"

"I can see Cheju-do like a pebble in the ocean!"

"I can see the stars spell out my name!"

Dawn began to leak over the horizon. Hye-yang rose and rose with the spreading light.

The inside of the windshield is hot as an electric blanket against my palm. It's easily over a hundred degrees outside the car. I click the air conditioner up a notch and begin to navigate another 168-mile loop around the Salton Sea, my third continuous circle in the past six hours: Highway 86 until it curves into the 195 near Oasis, until it curves into the 111 near Mecca, until it curves, at Brawley, back into the 86 again.

The sea glints beyond scrubby, cracked acres of desert. I see it out of the corner of my eye, but I can't quite convince myself to drive any closer. As long as I keep circling, I haven't committed to anything—my car is just following the pull of gravity, a small planet orbiting a wet oblong star.

Splintered telephone poles line the road, forked open by lightning or wind. Dust devils spiral lazily over empty fields. Farmland turns into trailer park turns into citrus grove turns into date farm turns into vast expanse of sand and grit and nothing, the whole valley ringed with dark mountain ranges, looming brown parentheses of earth. I had thought this was a resort town, but there is not a golf course or fancy spa anywhere in sight. Maybe they're hiding somewhere between the highway and the water. Maybe they've evaporated in the desert heat.

I find myself anticipating certain landmarks I've already passed twice—the ancient liquor shop near Bombay Beach, the rusted-out motorboat in a field by Salton City, the soldier rows of date trees near 100 Palms. I begin to predict the name of the next passage of sand and gravel that will course beneath the road—*Alki Wash, Bee Wash, Cedar, Frink, Butter Wash, Wister, Sand, Signal Wash, Polo, Skee, Salt Wash, Gravel, Bug, Cattail Wash*. Near the horizon, the road wavers—

the asphalt, the land around it smearing into oily waves of vapor. I feel slightly dizzy, like my own edges are blurring out into the desert air, coagulating into dark distant hills.

I didn't say good-bye to my mother before I left. I didn't have a chance—she wasn't home when I woke up. I waited around longer than I planned to, but she never came back. I was worried I wouldn't go at all if I didn't go soon, so I wrote a quick note and left it on the counter by the robin's egg shoebox. As I loaded my *chang'go* into the car, a small slip of paper tumbled out from beneath the strings. Four lines of poetry were written there, in my mother's hand:

That fall the wild geese flew so far south
they took the sky with them.

Stay just as far away as you can;
time will keep or lead you back.

I recognized the lines from a library book I had once checked out, a collection of Korean courtesan poems from the Chosun dynasty. She must've looked at the book, must have copied some of the poems down, without me knowing. The thought of her reading those poems, poems written by *kisaeng,* women who had been used and ostracized by society six, seven centuries ago, was almost too much to handle. I put the poem in my pocket, loaded up the car, and pointed it, eyes brimming, toward the Salton Sea.

I have no idea how long I'll be gone—one week? A month? Long enough to try to set things right—whatever that means—if only I can bring myself close enough to the birds in the first place. The sea sparkles in my peripheral vision like a mirage. I know I can't keep circling like this, but for now it's all I can do.

Parakeet, Blue (Name: Lee Lee)

Ava, daughter, 13. Kill bird.
Forget to close cage after clean.
Lee Lee fly out window, into sky. Good bird,
like to eat seed in my mouth.
Songs in morning. No words.
Find him on patio, smack himself
dead on glass to get back in.

[birdseed captured under cellophane tape]

[pale blue feathers]

[bit of soiled Korean language newspaper]

2/11/84

Highway 111, as I come to know it, seems appropriately numbered—a row of three thin digits, each one almost invisible, spare and pale as the landscape it cuts through. Scattered patches of white—salt, I guess—gleam dully from the dirt like snow. Even the sky seems white, as if the blue had been taken by geese flying south, or, more likely, burned blank by the relentless sun.

I feel incredibly conspicuous in my shiny green car. The only other color along this stretch of the road comes from the occasional string of boxcars stopped on the Southern Pacific railway. The trains are pretty muted, too—dusty wine, dirty mustard, black sandstormed down to gray. The few cars I pass are equally eroded—pickup trucks painted with primer, twenty-year-old weather-faded sedans, eyes trained on me from inside, loaded with curiosity and threat. If I don't make some sort of decision soon, I worry that my own car, my own face might get sanded down to dust.

I crank the steering wheel and veer off the highway onto Desert Beach Drive.

The water spreads out before me, miles of flat shimmer. It looks refreshing, but as soon as I get out of the car, the heat and stench almost knock me over. An overpowering smell of bird and fish decay mixes in the air with something equally rank and environmental. I grab a piece of ginger to try to mask the scent, but the odor molecules still find a way to seep inside.

What planet have I landed on? I stomp a sleeping foot against the pavement, slap some life into my face, look around to make sure no cars have pulled into the lot behind me. The area is completely deserted. An empty fifties-style motel sits on the other end of the parking lot, all of its doors open, the rooms bare. The building is so utterly abandoned, no one has even bothered to vandalize it. Dusty tufts of overgrown bougainvillea seem incongruous against the walls, random bursts of fuchsia life.

A marina up ahead, partly underwater and long deserted, touts sandwiches and live bait from its sun-bleached awning. An old yacht club, shaped like a ship with broken porthole windows and faded nautical flags painted around the border, silently faces the water. It looks like no one has dined or danced there in decades. What happened here? *What happened?*

Holding my breath, I walk toward the sweeping span of water. As I get closer, the sea begins to looks less sparkly—it is the color of tea, the color of mud. The beach is not a sandy one, either, as it had seemed from the parking lot. The ground is completely heaped with barnacles, small white tubes that crunch beneath my sandals, making me shiver even in the intense heat. I remember reading somewhere that barnacles had been introduced to the area by WWII aircraft that used the sea for dive bomb practice. I feel like I'm walking across a bone yard.

Every few steps, I come across dead fish in various stages of decomposition—some still silver and wet with missing eyes, some dry and brown like the cuttlefish my mother buys in Koreatown, some dissolved down to bone, bleached white as the barnacles beneath them. Pale-green bird droppings offer the only other color on the ground. I walk up to an old swing set and steady myself against one of its hot metal legs. The end of a small slide disappears into a mass of barnacles nearby.

What am I doing here? I wonder, queasy from the rotten air. Then I see the jetty up ahead, covered with dead and dying pelicans.

The birds, dozens of them, are heaped against each other, a seething clump of beige and brown, long beaks jutting out like cactus spines. Some pelicans convulse violently, others have already started to decompose, their speckled breasts caved, split open. My eyes feel seared. Bile rises in my throat. I don't know what I expected—some ballet of languid wings, something remotely beautiful. Anything but this.

One bird lets out a horrible screech. Its head lifts briefly off the ground, then collapses, its beak wide open. I bend over and retch a small splash of orange onto the barnacles and fish bones, my contribution of color to the landscape.

I stumble back to the Sonata and blast the cold scent of Freon into my nose. My throat, my eyes are raw. I pop another sugary clump of ginger into my mouth, lean my head against the steering wheel, and take some deep breaths. It would be so easy to go home, so easy to hit the road and never look back. It would be so easy, but when I pull back onto the 111, I can't seem to drive toward San Diego. I find myself pulling off the highway again onto a street not far down the road, one I've passed three times already, a driveway with a sign that reads VISITOR'S CENTER.

I avoid the stuffed-animal displays inside the deeply air-conditioned building—my stomach feels wrung out like a rag; the glassy eye of a barn owl could easily twist me dry. A short, stocky woman behind the information counter, her face deeply creased by years of sun, looks up as she straightens a display of maps that look like they were printed at least three decades before.

"Can I help you?" Her voice is gravelly, cigarette-thick. She stares at me suspiciously.

"I'm here to help the birds?" I swallow the sweet acid that wants to rise up my throat again.

"You with Fish and Game?" the woman asks.

I shake my head.

"Fish and Wildlife?"

I shake my head again.

"Bureau of Land Management?"

"No . . ."

"The prison?"

"No!" I shake my head more emphatically.

"We're getting people from all over." The woman spreads her thick arms out to encompass them all. "Where'd you say you were from?"

"San Diego." I cough out the words.

"Oh, so you're from Sea World, then!" The woman's wrinkled face brightens. "I heard they were coming down to get some of the pelicans. I just love Sea World . . . took my friend's grandkids there not a month ago. Shamu had some kind of infection. Kids were mighty disappointed—show was canceled. How's he doing now?"

"I don't know . . ."

"Oh, of course not—you work with birds, not whales. Those flamingos you got are something else, aren't they?"

"Actually . . ."

"Can you imagine sleeping on one foot like that? I don't know how they keep their balance."

I shrug. I feel off balance on two feet.

"My friend's granddaughter wants to dye her hair like a flamingo . . . you think they dye those birds? Some looked pinker than others."

"Maybe . . ."

"And those penguins—aren't they darling? Like little Charlie Chaplins . . ." The woman starts to waddle around in imitation behind her desk.

"I'm not from Sea World," I finally blurt out.

The woman stops her penguin walk. She looks crestfallen, as if I had deliberately misled her. Her gaze turns suspicious again.

"I'm here on my own," I tell her. "I figured they'd need more volunteers . . ."

The woman takes a moment to compose herself. "You want to speak to Darryl Sternberg over at the hospital." Her voice is suddenly businesslike, her face flushed.

"And where would that be?" I ask.

"Just beyond the dock we got out back, and up the beach a ways." She busies herself again with her map straightening.

"Thank you." I dig into my pocket, hand a dollar to the woman, then take a map from the front of the display. The woman nods curtly before the whole display stand tumbles over again. I start to help her pick up the maps.

"You better go see Darryl before it gets too hot," she says. "It got up to one-twenty yesterday. He's gonna be cranky."

"Thank you," I tell her. "I'm sorry about this . . ."

The woman nods and slaps the maps together as I take a sip

from a water fountain to soothe my aching throat before I walk back out into the blast of heat outside.

A temporary structure is set up a few hundred yards ahead on the barnacled shore—chain-link walls covered with UV-protectant fabric. The air gets heavier, thick with the scent of something gone wrong, as I get closer. My stomach twists tighter.

Through the opening between two of the chain-link panels, I can see at least fifty people inside. Some tend pelicans in a child's wading pool, others unload trash bags full of dead birds. Some weigh the birds, catalog them, slit their bellies open, put hearts and livers into clear sandwich bags. In a small red tin structure adjacent to the enclosure, two men throw bodies into an incinerator that sends more heat into the sweltering air. A pile of dead birds taller than me stands in the corner. The stench is unbearable. I fan myself with the folded map.

"Can I help you?" A harried-looking man comes up to me.

"I'm looking for the hospital."

"You found it," he replies, then races off to the plastic pool full of birds, syringes of some kind spilling out of his vest pockets.

"This is the hospital?" I ask another man who is hefting a dead pelican onto a scale.

"You were expecting private beds?" he asks as he records the weight, then throws the bird in a pile.

"Running water, maybe." I look around. No sink, no fans. Dirt floor. Flies everywhere.

The man laughs and points to a long hose that snakes across the ground.

"Could you please tell me where I could find Darryl?"

"He's over there." He points to the man by the wading pool, the man I had first talked to.

"Thank you." I try not to breathe. My voice sounds the way I've heard people speak after they've inhaled pot, all tight in the throat.

I walk over to the pool. A woman holds a pelican's floppy neck while Darryl squirts something from one of the syringes through a tube into its beak.

"Excuse me." I tentatively tap his shoulder.

He snaps his head around. Part of the liquid from the syringe squirts out, splashes against my jeans.

"Dammit!" he shouts.

"I'm sorry . . ."

"That syringe was measured out perfectly," he says. "This bird only got about sixty milliliters of electrolytes, thanks to you. Those forty milliliters on your calf aren't going to do you any good, are they?"

"I didn't mean—"

"Who *are* you?"

"My name is Ava. Ava Sing Lo. I'm here to help the birds."

"Well, then." He hands me a wet cloth. It is blessedly cool in my palm. He gestures to a pelican sitting at the edge of the pool, its neck draped languidly over the edge. "Wipe out this bird's eyes. I need to get more solution." He storms off.

I tuck my map into my pocket. "What do I do?" I ask the woman, stroking a pelican's head. The woman's light-brown hair is starting to come out of its hasty ponytail. Sweat streams down her forehead, trickles behind her glasses, down her freckled nose, over her chapped lips.

"Just wipe its eyes with the cloth," she says. "They fall down and can't hold up their heads, poor things. Their eyes get all full of mud and salt and crap before we can get to them . . ."

I swallow and walk to the other side of the blue plastic pool, which I now realize has circus animals printed all over it, almost mockingly festive. I kneel down beside the bird. Its eyes are so caked, I'm sure it can't see a thing. I tentatively raise the cloth to the pelican's head. I can feel the bird startle a bit, but it is too weak to do much. I gently touch the cloth against its covered eye. The bird flinches, shudders. A wing brushes lightly against my arm, sends a shiver down my spine. I wipe at the hardened crud, then run some water from the hose over the cloth so that I can loosen it some more. Eventually the dirt smears off. The pelican's eye looks right into mine. My heart starts to pound.

"It's okay," I tell the bird, then move over to the other side. The bird relaxes a bit as I wipe at the other eye. Once that one emerges from the layers of mud and salt, though, it is glassy, vacant. It takes me a moment to realize the pelican is dead.

"Oh, no," I whisper.

"We lose a lot of them," the woman says, raising her arm as if to signal someone.

"I have sort of a history of killing birds," I tell her.

The woman doesn't say anything, but I can feel her recoil.

A man in an olive-drab jumpsuit comes up to the pool and whisks the bird away without a word.

"How can you stand this?" I ask the woman.

"It doesn't get any easier," the woman admits. "Believe me."

"Are you a volunteer?"

"No, I'm with a wildlife refuge in Colorado. They shipped a few of us out here to help with the effort. I'm supposed to be here another two weeks, but frankly, I'm not sure I can hang on that long."

I wonder how long I can stand it myself. It would be so easy to just walk away. I know I can't, though, not yet.

"How many birds have been affected so far?"

"Over three thousand already—a few hundred brown pelicans among them. They're endangered, you know. It's kind of ironic, really—earlier this year, the browns were getting close to getting off the list, but now with this outbreak, it's possible we'll have to add the western whites to the list now, too."

I look around. The pile of dead birds is almost too awful to comprehend, big enough to fill the pages of several scrapbooks.

"I'm Abby, by the way," the woman extends her hand. "Abby Westin."

"Ava Sing Lo."

Abby's fingers are waterlogged and wrinkled against the back of my hand.

"Where are you staying?" Abby asks.

"I'm not sure. This whole thing was sort of a split-second decision. I figured I would find something once I got here."

"There aren't any hotels nearby," Abby says. "Not anymore, at least."

"I saw the one off Desert Beach Drive. It's like a ghost town over there."

"It's like a ghost town everywhere," says Abby. "If you want, you can bunk with me. They've set up big army tents for all the people who've traveled here to help."

"I'm just a volunteer."

"I'm sure you could stay with me," says Abby. "There's an empty cot. The gal who was sharing the place couldn't deal with all this. I was this close to leaving with her."

"No time for chitchat, girls." Darryl reappears. "We have to tube these birds. The van from the Pacific Wildlife Center is going to be here any moment to bring them to Laguna Niguel."

"What do they do with them there?" I ask.

"Rehabilitate them some more," he says, as he sticks a tube into a pelican's beak. The pelican is weak, but it has enough gumption to give him a bit of a struggle. "More electrolytes, then a multi milk solution—half milk, half water—eventually fish. When they're strong enough, up and preening, they get released." He hands Abby a tubed syringe. I watch her feed it to a pelican easily, like she has done it hundreds of times. She probably has.

"Darryl," asks Abby. "Would it be possible for Ava to bunk with me? She's not with the refuge—she's here as a volunteer—but she needs a place to stay."

"Don't see why not." Darryl tubes another bird. "We appreciate your help—it's the least we could do in return—not that the accommodations are all that spectacular."

"That's fine," I tell him. "Thank you."

"Welcome aboard." Darryl tosses me a syringe.

An hour later, after I struggle, and fail, to tube several birds, Abby tells me about a weekly boat tour for new volunteers and refuge workers. If I hurry, she says, I can make it. I have a feeling she just wants to get rid of me, but Darryl says it's a good opportunity to get a sense of the sea's expanse, its history, its flora and fauna. I stumble to the dock, where I am shuttled onto a boat with about ten other shell-shocked people. They sit like zombies, silently facing each other on the two benches that stretch the length of the boat. My arms feel raked by resistant pelican beaks; my biceps sting, but I can't find any scratches when I examine my skin.

A perky woman in a tan uniform hops on board and starts up the motor. As the pontoon pulls out onto the sea, she launches into her regular tour spiel like she has a boat full of eager vacationers, not a group of death-stunned workers.

"The Salton Sea," she says grandly, "was created by mistake! In 1905, water diversion dikes along the Colorado River collapsed, and water flooded into the ancient Salton Basin for almost two years, leaving behind the largest inland lake in California! Today the lake is about thirty-five miles long and fifteen miles wide and straddles two counties! It boasts one of the best fisheries you could ever find!"

She rattles off the varieties of fish in the sea as if they're all swimming happily in the depths, ready to be snared by some lucky wrangler's hook. As if they're not bloated and wasted by botulism, clotting the surface of the water.

When she mentions that the tilapia originally came from Africa, the whole crowd in the boat mutely swivels around to face me, as if I'm responsible for the slew of fish myself. I look down, my face hot. Brownish water seeps up through some little grommeted holes on the floor of the boat and slides over to my feet. I tense my toes inside my shoes. When the woman says that tilapia are mouth brooders, that their babies swim into their parents' mouths for protection, I can feel everyone stare at my lips.

I don't hear much else until the woman mentions gulf croakers. The fish actually croak when they die, the woman says, as the pontoon journeys toward the center of the sea; they make a froglike croaking sound. When they're alive, they make a sound like a drum. It's because of their modified air bladders. The woman sounds a bit embarrassed by this last word.

I try to listen for the fish drum, fish croak, but all I can hear is the motor of the boat. I never knew fish could make sounds. I'll try to record some later for my MIDI, maybe mix them with Kane's voice. With all the dead fish floating around, I'll probably have a better chance hearing them croak than I will hearing them drum, although I would much prefer something percussive. My hands feel restless for the skin of my *chang'go.* I thrum my fingers against the edge of the boat until someone shoots me a dirty look.

I started drumming on my first birthday. I can't remember the actual event, but I remember my mother's telling of it.

In Korea it's traditional to have a huge first birthday feast, during which objects are set before the child—coins, a calligraphy brush, a dancer's fan. The first object the child reaches for supposedly determines his or her life's path.

That day, so the story goes, my mother brought me to McDonald's. She set a few things on the table—some pennies, a shell, a small doll, a comb—but I reached for the chopsticks my mother had brought from home. She had been using them to eat her french fries, dangling each strip of potato in front of her mouth like a worm before she bit it away from the pinch of wood. I grabbed the sticks right out of her hand and banged and banged them against the yellow Formica.

Table drum, floor drum, chair drum, bed drum, knee drum, eardrum, heart drum, *ba dum, ba dum,* the whole world became a drum for me that day. When I was three, I got my first real drum— a feathered tom-tom my mother bought at a dime store. When I was six, she found a used set of bongos at a garage sale. Then, when I turned eleven, my mother gave me the *chang'go,* the drum that quickly became my home, my heart. That night was the first night she sang the *pansori* to me, the first night she began to let her story spill. Sometimes I think my whole life has been a silence punctuated by drum beats and MIDI samples and tae kwon do grunts. In between, I feel blank as the desert sky. Only sound can pull me into sharp relief.

A loud motor, like wire brushes on cymbals, whirs into earshot. I look up as an airboat speeds by, its floor heaped with pelicans, a man in an orange jumpsuit standing above them. The sight of the birds is sickening, but the huge caged fan mounted on the back of the boat sends a welcome blast of slightly cooler air across my face as it passes. Out in the water, the air is not quite so stifling, the stink not quite so lethal, but it is still hotter and smellier than anything I'll ever be used to. I'm grateful to at least have some space around my head, some open sky, after being walled in at the bird hospital for the last hour. The mountains that ring the sea are too far away to feel like walls.

The woman points out the line that cuts across the hills like a belt. A waterline, she says, from an ancient sea. This basin has been filled many times, with both salt- and freshwater. Freshwater snail shells can still be found up there.

The pontoon passes the top of a telephone pole that juts out of the water like a thick finger. The water level, the woman explains, keeps rising because of agricultural runoff from nearby farms. The sea won't reach those watermarks up in the hills anytime soon, but it does sometimes rise enough to cause problems. Several resort areas were inundated in the seventies. Whole buildings are now underwater.

"The Salton Sea has no outlet!" she explains to her catatonic audience.

The phrase sounds incredibly foreboding, even though I know the sea could be just the outlet I've been looking for. The boat passes some dead treetops pushing up through the wet surface. The branches are covered with birds. Living birds. Common cormorants, says the woman.

These birds are diving birds, she says, great fishers, but they're clumsy on the ground. They jump off trees to fly so that they won't have to run. See their legs, way back on their bodies, like they're coming out of their rumps? They'd tip over if they tried to run. In the Orient, the woman continues, people keep these birds as pets.

I expect everyone to turn and look at me again, but no one does. I am amazed they can't see my mother shining through my skin. My whole body feels like a watermark, a dark salty line left behind by the unknown soldier who fathered me. Only my eyes, my cheekbones, carry traces of my mother, like snail shells left behind, fragile memories of freshwater.

That night, I leave the heat of the canvas tent I share with Abby in search of a phone. I follow a narrow trail, cut through some pungent-smelling brush, silvery in the beam of my flashlight. The trail ends at a wall of dirt, chest-high. When I walk up to it, I am startled to find water on the other side, mushrooming dark over the lip of earth. If the dirt barrier were to crumble, the sea would come pouring out, knocking me over. I turn and run back down the path, branches scratching at my clothes.

As I pass back through the encampment, I catch sight of the ranger station and find my way to the pay phone. From here, the sea looks flat, nonthreatening. I watch the water shimmer in the moonlight and let my breath return to normal as the answering machine clicks on in San Diego. My own generic "please leave a message" recording is gone, replaced by a squawk, then Kane's voice crowing, "*Yoboseyo?*"

I can't remember Kane ever saying the special phone hello before; I certainly can't remember recording it. Either my mother impersonated his voice on the tape or she bought another parrot. Both possibilities make me feel strange. So does the fact that my mother changed the message so quickly after I left.

"Omma?" I ask after the beep. "Are you home?" I picture my voice trailing out into the living room. "Hello? Are you there?"

No one picks up.

A train rattles in the distance.

"I'm at the Salton Sea, Omma." I try to raise my voice above the train's whistle. Hopefully my message will be audible. "I just wanted to let you know I got here okay. I helped out in the bird hospital for a while. Tomorrow they want me to walk around the beaches to find more birds. Hopefully I'll find some that can be saved. I don't know how—"

The answering machine beeps and cuts me off. I consider calling back, but I'm not sure what else I would say. The trains keep coming.

The tent is like a sauna when I enter it, shining my flashlight ahead of me. Abby, asleep in her clothes, frowns and flips over when the light hits her face. I flick it off and find my way to my cot in the dark. I strip down to my underwear, fold the hot top blanket down to the bottom of the cot and scoot under the scratchy sheet beneath. It takes me a long time to fall asleep. Right after I finally drift off, around 2:00 A.M., Abby cries out in her sleep. I wake up, heart pounding.

"Omma?" I ask, ready to grab my drum. Then the heat hits me, the smell, and I remember where I am. I wait for my heart to calm down, wait for it to feel steady as the trains that seem to run all night, a rhythm of steel against track that echoes across the hills. I slide back into sleep, clack clack, clack clack. Every couple of hours, Abby cries out again.

Dried squid dangled around Hye-yang's head like stiff mittens from clothesline strings. The flat brown bodies brushed against the tips of her ears, her forehead, her hair, as she navigated her way around the stand. She enjoyed selling the cuttlefish to hungry Folk Village visitors, but after a few weeks, she began to feel restless in her little booth, tired of the fish reek that began to waft from her skin. During a lull, she wandered over to the archery area, picked up a bow, and shot an arrow straight into the heart of the rice straw target. A manager saw; one of his archers was going to marry a GI and leave the village, he said. Would she be willing to perform demonstrations? Hye-yang was quick to accept the offer. She saw the squid lift off her skin by the dozens, a whoosh of leathery wings in flight.

She soon spent long, satisfying hours pulling her right arm back, squinting her eyes into fierce focus. All the shame she had caused her family on the island distilled into one thin, sharp point after another, then flew straight out of her arms.

At Sun's urging, Hye-yang also began to sing a few times a week. She sang most often for the traditional farmer's dance troupe, but her true moment of glory came when she was allowed to sing the *pansori,* accompanied by a single drum. Her voice wasn't ripped raw like a trained *pansori* singer's, but she could feel lament and longing thick in her throat. She knew the crowd could feel it, too—she often saw men and women cry when she sang. Their tears fed her, filled her heart near to bursting with wet diamond drops. Her whole body sometimes felt ready to explode into song, shimmering like a handful of glitter in the air.

Every night, she and Sun pushed their sleeping mats together; their hair, their hands tangled like dreams as they slept. Every day, Hye-yang woke up eager to go to work. She never felt so happy, so deeply at home in her life.

A year after Hye-yang arrived at the Folk Village, Sun planned a trip back to Cheju-do for her grandmother's sixtieth birthday celebration. Hye-yang felt torn. She missed the island, missed the jagged cliffs, the salt air, the fields of yellow rapeseed flowers, but she hadn't heard from her mother and grandmother since she left. The only time she let herself remember their faces was when she wrote their names across the envelope she sent home each month with a portion of her earnings. The women often appeared in her dreams, though, swimming deep underwater, grabbing at strange sea creatures. When she tried to reach for them, they dissipated like clouds.

A storm brewed while Hye-yang watched her friend pack for the weekend. Rain began to explode against the ground as soon as Sun kissed Hye-yang good-bye and left the dormitory. Through the window, Hye-yang watched Sun bend against the wind while she made her way toward the bus station. With weather like this, Hye-yang knew she wouldn't be able to perform outdoors at the Folk Village for days, with either her bow or her voice. She would have to spend the weekend shivering in the cuttlefish stand, water dripping through the straw roof, turning the strands of squid slick and even more pungent. Hye-yang suddenly realized how empty the Folk Village would feel without Sun around. She grabbed some clothes, threw them into a small bag, and ran through the storm to catch up with her friend.

Peach face lovebirds (2) (Names: Lulu, Soo)
Ava, daughter, 21. Kill birds with pan.
She buy me pan at flea market for scrambled egg.
When she cook it, birds fall down. Gas comes from pan
(called Teflon). Smells like nothing to person,
make birds into nothing.

[small feathers, lime green and peach]

[foil wrapper from stick of butter]

[receipt from flea market]

7/18/93

I walk along the beaches, my hands stuffed into hot gloves, garbage bags sweating against my legs. A week on the job, I have yet to find a living bird among the barnacles, but there is no shortage of dead ones. Every couple of hours, another one of my bags is full, bulging with feathers and bones. Beaks strain against the plastic; some poke all the way through. I leave the bags on the beach so someone from the hospital can pick them up later in a golf cart. The heat and stench that permeate each hour of my day slowly become familiar, but never less disturbing.

After dinner, Darryl suggests we all have a scent party to get the death smell out of our noses. Everyone rushes off to their tents and comes back with various bottles and cans and candles and baggies to put on the picnic table. We all circle it, leaning over to sniff the various objects, walking slowly, hesitantly, like we're playing musical chairs.

I deeply inhale Old Spice deodorant, a stick-on air freshener disk, a bayberry scented candle, a handful of eucalyptus seeds, citronella insect repellent. I can feel Darryl's eyes linger on me as I bend over an unlit incense cone, a plastic jug of baby wipes, a tube of coconut suntan oil. The way he looks at me has changed since I've been here—his eyes turn soft in my direction. My shoulders tense, and I feel him turn away, but our heads knock into each other as we both lean toward a lavender-scented sachet. I jump back, bumping Abby's face into a jar of instant coffee. When Abby lifts her head, her nose is coated in brown powder.

"Sorry," Darryl and I both say at the same time. I don't look at him, but I can feel him hesitate for a moment, then move further ahead, toward some cedar chips, anise-flavored toothpaste, rose-petal potpourri.

"No problem," laughs Abby, brushing herself off. "I love the smell of coffee."

She plunges a finger into a pot of Vicks VapoRub and smears it under my nose.

The menthol fills my skull, cools my face, burns the touch of Darryl's eyes off my skin. I can barely smell the packet of Kool-Aid, ripped open, or the paper wrapper that once held salt taffy that comes next. I rub some of the slick goo off my upper lip. When I look up again, Darryl is gone.

I stumble, scent-drunk, back to the tent and pull the small box of candied ginger from my purse. I almost brought the box to the scent party but in the end decided not to. The ginger is for me alone. I didn't want it to get touched, changed, by so many other smells. I crush a bit between my fingers and breathe in the sharp scent of it, like smelling salts, to clear my swooning, aroma-swimming head.

"I think Darryl likes you," Abby says as she comes into the tent, a few dark grains still on her nose.

"I don't want to be liked right now." I pop a piece of ginger into my mouth, then close my eyes, heart pounding.

"Do you have a boyfriend at home?" asks Abby.

I shake my head.

"A girlfriend?"

"No." I open my eyes again.

"Darryl's a nice guy." Abby takes off her shirt and rubs her face with it.

"I know. I just don't want to get involved with anyone right now." I don't tell Abby that I've never really been involved with anyone before—just a few ridiculous dates in college. I don't tell her that I'm scared my mother will rise up like a ghost between me and anyone I try to touch, that she'll get between me and any pleasure I may hope to feel. I don't tell her my nipples are inverted, the tips sucked back into my chest like a turtle pulling its head back into its shell, like something shying away from the light. I don't tell her that whenever I touch myself, whenever I try to bring myself to that place of shiver and sigh I've heard so much about, my mother's voice shrieks inside my head and my body shuts down. I don't tell her my mother's story is so heavy in my bones that I can't even begin to think about writing a new story for myself.

"Good night, Ava." Abby slips into her cot.

"Sweet dreams," I tell her, although I'm sure they'll be anything but. I try not to think about Darryl trying to sleep, maybe thinking of me, just a few yards away.

I can see my mother's heart. It glows inside her chest in the dark, a hummingbird feeder filled with bright-red liquid. Two tubes swoop out from the bottom; the rubber tips poke through the droop of her breasts. I bend and wrap my lips around one. The hollow pellet is hard, like a bead on a cheap necklace. I press it between my palate and tongue and begin to suck. A thin, sweet liquid pours into my mouth. Hungry, I pull harder with my tongue, but only a feeble stream flows out. My mother's rib cage contracts—painfully, it appears—with each vacuum pull of my mouth. The hummingbird feeder rattles inside. I can tell if I suck too hard, the glass will shatter. I relax my lips and pull away. My mother spins around and walks back into the night.

I wake up starving, a film of sweetness on my tongue. I don't feel hungry, exactly—more hollowed out, like some of the birds I find, ones that have been gutted by wild dogs or the steady jaw of decomposition. My appetite has been gone for days, so I am glad to feel some semblance of hunger, but at breakfast I can barely swallow down a bite or two from a tin of military-issue corned beef hash. I don't think I can stomach eating near the hospital anymore. I can't stomach eating with people who handle dead birds, can't stomach these Meals Ready to Eat, the containers sealed like small coffins. Maybe if I could find a real meal, one made with actual fresh ingredients, I'd be able to force something down.

By lunchtime, the heat is so unbearable, it almost takes away my appetite, but I ask for some suggestions anyway.

"There's a place out by Bombay Beach, just south of here," Darryl says. "I've heard it's pretty good."

"Maybe I'll give it a try." I look at my feet.

"Would you like some company?" he asks.

I feel myself blush.

"No, thanks," I tell him. "I just need to get away by myself for a little bit."

"I know the feeling," he says. "But I probably need to stay here, anyway—I am Mr. Supervisor Man, after all." He affects a superhero pose—legs out wide, hands on hips, chest puffed out.

I pretend not to notice his stance. "I'll tell you all about it."

Darryl's chest deflates, his arms drop.

"Bon appetit!" he calls out as I walk to my car.

* * *

In the rearview mirror, I watch Darryl watch me drive away. I shift my thoughts to the road ahead, the familiar blankness of the 111, the heat that the air conditioner can't quite seem to dispel. I wonder if Bombay Beach is an East Indian colony, although I can't imagine people in saris at the Salton Sea, eating samosas and chewing on cardamom seeds. After all, Mecca Beach certainly isn't an Islamic spiritual destination. Still, I find myself excited by the prospect of some real food. Even more excited by the prospect of getting away from the birds, the bird people, Darryl's slow warm gaze.

The Aloha Room sits in the middle of a salt-encrusted parking lot near the water. Inside, the air is blessedly cool and smells blessedly clean—no trace of bird. Hawaii memorabilia straight out of the fifties is tacked to bamboo-lined walls, interspersed with photos of John Wayne and other Hollywood cowboys. Neon beer signs sputter their light into the dim room, along with the paper Japanese lanterns in orange and green and pink that hang from the ceiling. A counter spans one wall by the kitchen, shaded by an awning made of straw. Red and black vinyl booths line the other walls. A revolving pie rack gleams near the cash register, peaks of meringue rising inside like clouds. I feel my mouth begin to water for the first time in days.

In one booth, a woman, the only customer in the restaurant, sits hunched over a cigarette. I glance at her offhandedly, then do a double take. She appears to be wearing a tiara and a huge plush tomato costume. I wonder if I'm hallucinating from lack of sleep, but even after I rub my eyes, the woman is still in the strange outfit, along with black fishnet stockings and bright-red pumps.

"Hey, Miss Tomato!" a heavyset woman with salmon-colored hair calls out from the kitchen window that opens out to the counter. "Show some vegetable spirit, why don't you?"

"A tomato is a *fruit*," Miss Tomato answers sullenly, her voice raspy, as far from a tomato voice as I could have imagined. "You should know that, Frieda, you work in the food service industry."

The woman steps out from behind the counter and walks over to where I'm standing by the front door, unsure whether or not to seat myself or wait for some sort of permission.

"She won the Miss Tomato Pageant at the Tomato Festival over in Niland today, and is she celebrating?" She gestures to the woman in the booth. "Is she whipping herself into one big salsa party? No, Miss Tomato Emily Lawrence is moping around the Aloha Room like a great big rotten vegetable."

"Fruit, Frieda!" Miss Tomato repeats before she takes another big drag on her cigarette. "I wouldn't be no stinking vegetable."

"Are you from the health board?" Frieda asks. I shake my head.

"You should put out that ciggy anyway, Emily," says Frieda. "I don't want to get busted. You're not supposed to be smoking in here."

Emily gives her the finger and takes another drag.

"Have a seat," says Frieda.

I walk over to a duct-taped counter stool. The woman presents a coffee-and-grease-stained menu with a flourish.

"Specials today are patty melt with chips, breaded veal cutlet, and Cobb salad, except with no ham, but I could do double turkey."

"Veal is cruel, Frieda." Emily gets up from her booth and squeezes herself into a stool two away from me. Some of the soft tomato costume smooshes over, presses into my elbow. I'm seized with the urge to wrap my arms around it like a big stuffed animal and fall asleep. "You know what they do to make veal? They lock poor little baby cows up in cages and don't even let them walk around or nothing."

"Well, I don't do *that*." Frieda shakes her head knowingly at me. "We buy them frozen from the Price Club."

The tomato woman snorts and takes another puff. "Give me a Bud," she says. "Lite."

"I always did like pickled tomatoes." Frieda winks before she shooshes the beer from the tap into a large plastic glass and hands it to Emily.

"You would think he would at least show up for the pageant." The tomato woman turns to me, her tiara slightly askew on her bleach-blonde hair. Dark roots sprout from her jagged part. "You would think that if he cared about me one friggin' iota, he would be there to see me at least do my tap dance number."

"Her boyfriend didn't show," Frieda says in a stage whisper.

"He's a Tomato Adjuster, for god's sake," Emily says. "All the tomato people got the day off."

"I'm sure he had a good excuse," I pipe up, suddenly aware I haven't said a word since I walked in.

"Oh, so you know where he went?" Emily scrunches her eyebrows at me. "You tell me, where the fuck was he?" She slams her cup against the counter. Beer sloshes out onto her costume, darkens and mats it in a series of blotches.

"I'm sorry . . ."

"Don't you pick on this poor girl," Frieda scolds Emily, then turns to me. "She's just pissed off, sweetheart. Don't you listen to her."

"He's probably off porking some other little tomato, the slime bucket." Emily guzzles the rest of her beer. "I owe you, Frieda," she says, then hefts herself off the stool and strides toward the door, red plush bobbing around her. It takes Emily a few tries to get out—the sides of the costume won't fit through the jamb. She has to turn sideways and scrunch the tomato with both of her hands before she can leave.

"What'll it be, honey?" Frieda asks.

I quickly scan the menu, my brain a bit addled from the tomato woman.

"The Cobb salad sounds fine." I point to the hand-printed specials paper-clipped to the menu.

"Good choice," the woman says, "even without the ham."

"Is she gone?" A man's voice booms out of the kitchen.

"It's safe, you can come out now," Frieda chimes back.

"Thank god." He pokes his head in the window.

"Oh, she's not that bad, Ray, come on." Frieda leans over rows of glasses to kiss him.

"She's a man-eater." Ray ducks out of the kitchen, rubbing his short salt-and-pepper beard with one hand, holding the large plastic salad bowl with the other. He wears the same kind of Hawaiian shirt that Frieda does. They are about the same size, too, in girth, the buttons straining against their bellies. "And I don't mean that in any pleasurable way." He sets the salad on the counter in front of me.

"I should hope not," Frieda laughs. "This is my husband, Ray," she tells me. "Ray, this is . . . I didn't ever get your name, did I?"

"Ava. Ava Sing Lo."

"Well, isn't that a pretty name, now?" Frieda says. "Sounds Oriental."

"Hmmm." I spear a cherry tomato.

"So, what brings you into these parts, Miss Ava Sing Lo?" asks Ray.

"The birds. I'm helping out at the hospital."

"Oh, isn't it a shame?" Frieda's face washes over with sadness. "It just about breaks my heart. Not so good for business, either. Just this morning, in fact, we carried about eight or so dead pelicans, and one tern, to the dumpster. They were just lying there on the parking lot by the beach."

"You should call the hospital about them," I tell her. "We're doing statistics, and we have an incinerator."

"Oh, I wouldn't want to get in the way of you doing your job, honey," says Frieda, "but we were about to open for breakfast and we sure didn't want to turn the stomachs of our customers. It's hard enough getting people to come here as it is, off the beaten track and all."

I force down the lettuce and strips of processed cheese I held in my mouth. These people had been carrying dead birds a few hours ago; who knew how well they washed their hands? My appetite quickly withers.

"And the smell—that's enough to turn them away," adds Ray.

I push my salad bowl toward a glass sugar container.

"It's worse even than the algae tides, and those can stink up the place like you don't want to know," says Frieda. "Which do you think is worse, Ray? The green tides or the red?"

"Nothing stinks like these birds." He pinches his nose. "But you get used to it, you know, just like you can get used to pretty much anything." He leans his elbow on the counter; an anchor is tattooed on the inside of his forearm. POPEYE, I think, even though Ray's arms are not nearly as big as the cartoon character's, and both his eyes seem serviceable.

"I think the green tides are worse than the red." Frieda scrunches up her face. "The green are algae, the red are little dinosaur germs."

"Dinoflagellates," Ray corrects.

"They turn the whole sea red, or green, depending on the tide. Sometimes it gets so bad, all the oxygen gets sucked out of the water. People come and load all the fish on big trucks so they won't suffocate."

"Where do they bring them?" I ask.

"Don't rightly know—some big pond somewhere? They bring them back when the tide dies down. There's always plenty of fish here."

"Looks like there might not be too many after this die-off," I say. "There's more dead fish than birds, I think."

"Is that so? That's a shame, truly. I guess I've heard that if the water keeps getting saltier, the fish might not survive too much longer anyway."

"This is some kind of place." Ray tugs at his beard. "It's amazing anything can survive out here at all."

"But we do, babe, don't we?" Frieda pinches his stomach.

"That we do." He smiles at her. "Barely," he adds, looking at me. I suddenly feel guilty and dig into my pocket for enough money to cover the tab.

"So where do you hail from, sweetheart?" Frieda asks as Ray wanders back to the kitchen. "I'll bet it's someplace exotic—you look a little like some of the girls we have on the wall here. Are you from Hawaii?"

"San Diego, actually." I put some crumpled bills on the counter.

"Where you staying?" Frieda ignores the money. I feel self-conscious about it and lay my palm over the dollars, so just small edges poke out, like my hand is on a bed of lettuce.

"I'm sharing a tent with one of the rescue workers," I tell her. "I haven't been sleeping much, though. My roommate has bad dreams. Screaming dreams."

"That's no surprise," says Frieda. "It's a real nightmare out there."

"I hope I'll be able to stay awake." I try to stifle a yawn.

"Honey," Frieda says. "If you need a place to stay, we got a trailer you could use."

I cock an eyebrow.

"I have an old double-wide here in Bombay that's just sitting there empty. I haven't lived there in years, myself. My sister stayed in it for a while, but she moved to Arizona a couple of months ago. You'll like the place—it has a view and everything. Just needs a little airing out."

I bite my lip, which tastes disturbingly of turkey juice, and take another sip of water. "I don't know . . ."

"It's paid for already, so it's not like we really need a rental income or anything," says Frieda, "so long as you eat here every so often and don't trash the place. Utilities are up to you, too, of course."

"Of course." I nod, mulling it over. "It's very generous of you to offer—I suppose I could at least take a look at it."

"It's nothing." Frieda winks as she slides the bills out from under my hand. "You done with that rabbit food?"

I nod again.

"Well, then. Let's skedaddle!" Frieda hits the counter with her palm. "Ray, I'm taking Miss Ava Sing Lo here out to see the double-wide!" she calls as she ducks under the counter door.

"Hurry back, sweet cakes," Ray says with a deadpan voice, as Frieda grabs me excitedly by the elbow and leads me to the door.

"I'd already forgotten how hot it is out here." I squint as we blast out into the sunlight. In the heat, I feel like Miss Tomato myself, encased in a huge, sweaty orb of fake fur. "You have a good air conditioner in there."

"*Refrigerated air,*" nods Frieda. "We make sure to put that on all of our signs." She leads me to her car, a white Nova, at least twenty years old.

"I haven't really been around Bombay Beach yet," I tell her as she pulls her seat belt across her lap. "All I've seen so far is your restaurant."

"There isn't a whole lot to it." The car chugs through the salty lot.

I adjust the vent on the dash, but all it does is pour out hot air.

"It takes a while for the AC to kick in," says Frieda.

Sweat trickles down my face as I look out the window. A few people are, unimaginably, fishing at a small inlet. As the car turns the corner, I see huge piles of dirt, at least ten feet tall, heaped up along the length of the shore. KEEP OFF SIDES OF DIKE USE STEPS say signs every few feet. Obviously people haven't been paying much attention. The dikes are crumbling in places, loose dirt scattered everywhere.

"Why are these here?"

"The water just keeps rising," Frieda says. "This town is actually below the water level right now—if you look on the other side of that dike, the water would be up to your navel, at least. It's all the runoff from the farms and everything—it keeps making the sea grow taller."

"Are people worried the town is going to get flooded?"

"Well, the dike's been holding up pretty good," says Frieda, "but lots do get washed out sometimes. If you look around later, you'll see there's a whole trailer park half underwater, all rusted out on the other side of the dike—kind of creepy. A hardware store's underwater, too, and a bait shop. Pigeons live there now. Did you know we have pigeons around here—just like a real city!"

I haven't seen any pigeons come into the hospital so far; I wonder if they've been affected at all by the die-off.

"See how all these trailers have platforms built on top of them?" Frieda asks.

Some trailers do indeed have small porches hoisted up over the roofs, some covered with Astroturf and plastic lawn furniture.

"Those places used to be primo property—you used to be able to see the water right out your window—but after the water went up and they put up the dikes, all you can see anymore is a load of dirt unless you put up a platform."

"You said your place has a view. How'd you manage that?"

Frieda just grins.

We drive a few more blocks, past empty lots covered with abandoned salt-encrusted boats and trailers. There are a few small cinder block houses, but most of the homes are trailers, most of them pretty rusty, their gravel yards full of dune buggies and shabby golf carts and old car parts. There are few lawns, fewer flowers, although there

is quite a bit of cactus, and many chain-link fences have an assortment of flat, sandy-looking stones propped up against them. We
drive by a hot-pink trailer with white iron scrollwork and a green
gravel lot full of lawn ornaments, which I instinctively know is
Emily's. Sure enough, Miss Tomato, out of her costume, although still
in fishnets and red high heels beneath her white shorts and striped
tube top, comes out onto the front steps and waves her cigarette at
us. Frieda honks and waves back. Emily does a little tap dance, wiggles her hips, sticks out her tongue, and disappears back inside her
house. Frieda laughs and shakes her head.

Could I actually live here? I wonder this even more as Frieda
turns another corner and eases the car into a driveway. I crane my
head to see out the windshield. Frieda's double-wide doesn't have
a platform erected over it. The whole trailer itself has been somehow hoisted up onto a platform, eight feet or so up in the air.

"Pretty nifty, huh?" Frieda says as we get out of the car.

"How did you do that?" I tilt my head back to take it all in.

"Boat hoist," Frieda says. "A friend of ours works at the marina.
Another friend works at the railroad—he got us the tracks for the
substructure, here . . ."

The frame of the platform does indeed appear to be built of
railroad tracks.

"And the railroad ties for the planking."

"These boards?" I look up at the slightly greasy-looking wood.

"They're the best," Frieda says. "They're soaked in pitch, so
they're weatherproof. Won't rot or nothing, ever. Some black stuff
oozes out of them sometimes, so just wear shoes when you go outside."

"Wow." I walk around under the platform, around the cast-iron
sewer pipe and copper water pipes and gray electrical conduit that
reach from the platform into the ground. "Are you sure this place
is safe?"

"The safest," Frieda says. "We went through that big quake a few years ago in there. Could barely feel it sway."

I walk back out from under it and look up. "What's that?" I point to a large metal tray that hangs off the edge of the platform.

Frieda unlocks a small metal box attached to one of the railroad tracks and pushes a button inside. The tray lowers down on pulleys until it is knee level in front of me.

"It's for groceries, luggage, what have you," says Frieda. "It could probably even lift you up there, but don't overdo it—I'm not sure how sound the motor is right now. The ladder is probably the best bet for you, yourself, but feel free to use the lift for your stuff. I'll give you the key."

"Can I take a look inside?" I can't tell if I'm fascinated or scared by the place. I can't quite imagine living inside of it.

"Of course." Frieda starts up the ladder. I follow her. A drop of sweat peels down Frieda's back, drops out the tail of her Hawaiian shirt, and hits me squarely on the nose. I want to wipe it off but feel too unsteady on the ladder to take my hand away. I turn my head and rub my face, as best I can, on my shoulder.

"It does need some airing out, like I said," Frieda says as she climbs up onto the platform and fumbles with the keys. I pull myself up behind Frieda. There isn't much room on the platform—about two feet sticking out from the trailer on all sides—and no railing. I feel a wave of vertigo. I move beside Frieda and steady myself against a window.

Frieda opens the door. "Phew," she says. "It smells like an old thermos in here."

It does smell a bit like old milk in the trailer, mixed with dirty socks and rusted, liquefying, lettuce. Not as bad as dead bird, but close. I hold my breath. It is hot inside, too, stiflingly so. Frieda sets to opening up·windows and turning on fans.

"All the utilities should still be on," she says.

I go to the small kitchen sink and lift up the faucet lever. Water spurts a bit, hot, but soon it starts to flow and cool off. I run my wrists under the stream, wipe them across my forehead. The kitchen has dark wood cabinets, a microwave that was probably among the first on the market, and green, orange, and tan flowered wallpaper. I walk around the rest of the texturized shag carpet in the trailer. There's not too much furniture. A small breakfast nook right outside of the kitchen, an olive-green couch in the living room, a couple of end tables next to it, one boasting a faceted amber glass lamp with a nubby beige shade.

It wouldn't be so bad to live here; it would be nice to get away from Abby's shouts, away from Darryl tossing and turning in the next tent. I peer into the bedroom. An afghan stretches over a bare full-size mattress; the bed stand next to it holds a clock radio and a lamp like the one in the living room. A low dresser sits across the room. And, lo and behold, an air conditioner is mounted in the window. I run over and turn the knob. Cold air blasts against my face.

"I'll take it!" I yell to Frieda, who is in the bathroom. The toilet flushes, water runs, and Frieda walks into the room, smiling.

"Well, then. Welcome home, sweetheart!" She grabs my hands in her wet ones.

The ferry ride to Cheju-do was choppy, the clouds overhead threatening to burst open. Sun snored against Hye-yang's arm, but Hye-yang barely slept through the night crossing. As the first morning light crept into the sky, Hye-yang watched the island grow bigger and bigger on the horizon, rocky and dark, until it threatened to engulf the whole ocean. She shivered as the air filled with a light gray mist.

Sun's family came to greet her at the dock. They swallowed her up like some great organism, a human amoeba. Sun's head poked up over the crowd as she was being swept away.

"Are you coming with us?" she yelled to Hye-yang.

Hye-yang shook her head and waved her friend on. At the bus station, she had wired her family to tell them she was coming home for a visit. Even though her mother had told her to never come back, Hye-yang didn't believe she meant it—especially since she was contributing money to the family; more than she ever could have made as a diver.

After she stood in the drizzle for two hours, a dock worker just ending his shift offered to give her a ride. Drenched and grateful, Hye-yang climbed into his car. They drove in silence for the first few minutes. Then, on a precarious road that overlooked the ocean, the man suddenly stopped the car with a jerk and unzipped his pants. He pushed Hye-yang's head toward his lap, but she screamed and tried to get out of the car. He clamped her mouth with one hand and grabbed her left hand with the other. Crushing her knuckles, the man forced her to move her hand up and down over his semierect penis until he spurted all over the dashboard. With his pants wide open, he started the car again, one of his hands still tight over Hye-yang's mouth. She looked out the window as a gull swooped toward the water, then disappeared under its dark husk.

The scent of the man's semen hung in the car like a sour rain. Hye-yang thought she might throw up. She tried to bite his hand, but she couldn't move her mouth freely enough. When they were half a mile from her family home, the man leaned over Hye-yang, popped open the door, and shoved her out. She tumbled on the ground a few times before she landed on her side. The car showered her with dirt and pebbles as it peeled away.

Hye-yang sat, stunned. Her right leg and hip were badly scraped from the fall. In a daze, she brushed herself off, wiping her left hand repeatedly against her coarse skirt. She spit onto the ground several times before she stood up, but couldn't get the acrid taste of the man's hand off her lips.

Hye-yang limped down the dusty road. She ran her hand along the rough edge of the long, low volcanic rock wall until the skin started to scrape off her palm, but she couldn't get the memory of the man's body off her palm.

In the distance, she could see a cluster of new houses, their corrugated tin roofs glinting through the light rain like an optical illusion. The houses were painted candy colors—tangerine orange, sea blue—so bright, they hurt her teeth. She was surprised by how glad she was to finally see the muted stone and straw of her family's house.

All three poles were up at the front gate, one crossed over the other two. No one was home. Hye-yang squeezed awkwardly between two of the poles. Her hip and hand throbbed. The front door was locked, which surprised her—there had never been a lock on the door before. With a great deal of discomfort, she pulled herself through an open window and collapsed onto the stone floor.

The house looked much the same as it did when she left, except for a small transistor radio on a windowsill and a black rotary telephone that rested on the ground beside her. Hye-yang picked up the receiver and let it hum into her ear. She could barely remember her mother's voice. Her mother and grandmother must have bought these small concessions to technology with the money she sent home. She set the phone back on its cradle and curled her body around it.

Several hours later, Hye-yang woke up sore and hungry. It was dark, but her mother and grandmother were still not back. She washed her hands several times in a bucket of water and lit a fire, then tore into a bowl of rice that was crusting by the stove. When she found no other food in the house, Hye-yang remembered the jar of kimchi that her mother always kept buried by the back door. She dug the crock up in the dark, her hands aching, dirt working deep into her scrapes. The vinegary cabbage was still crunchy, so Hye-yang knew it hadn't been fermenting long. It tasted good— spicy and familiar—even though it burned her raw hand. For the next two days, it was all she had to eat.

Hye-yang limped down to the beach a couple of times each day to search the choppy water for a glimpse of her mother's bobbing head, her grandmother's white diving clothes. Nothing moved but the waves and the occasional swooping bird. Walking back home, Hye-yang once caught a glimpse of what looked like a familiar face in one of the new tangerine-colored houses. As soon as she walked closer, the face disappeared. When she knocked on the door, no one answered.

Hye-yang wrote down the number on her mother's phone before she met Sun at the ferry docks. Sun looked well fed, happy.

She offered Hye-yang a handful of warm chestnuts. Hye-yang held out her torn palm.

"What happened?" asked Sun, concerned, as Hye-yang devoured the nuts like a starved animal.

Hye-yang told Sun about her family's absence. When Sun asked about Hye-yang's limp, Hye-yang told her she hurt her hip sliding down a hill. She didn't mention the ride with the dock worker, but he loomed large in Hye-yang's mind, dirty in her hand. She looked nervously around the area, but couldn't identify him among the uniformed men by the ferry.

"You should have come to my house," said Sun.

"I didn't want to disturb your grandmother's celebration," Hye-yang told her. "It was time for your family to be together."

"You *are* family." Sun put her arm around Hye-yang. "You are always welcome at my home—you should have known that. I wish you had come. If I had only known, I would have pulled you with me by the hair."

They stood together in silence for a moment.

"This will cheer you up." Sun suddenly smiled. "I met a man yesterday. A man from Kunsan."

Sun showed Hye-yang a tattered, familiar-looking pink business card. Hye-yang's breath caught in her throat.

"'Wild Ting Nightclub Establishment,'" Sun read slowly. They had both picked up some English in Suwon. The village managers wanted U.S. Air Force business and offered cursory English lessons to all employees. Hye-yang squinted at the words. English did not come as readily to her as it did to Sun. The looped letters made her dizzy. The skin on her chest began to burn.

"He told me I could be a famous dancer," said Sun. "He said many entertainment scouts from Hollywood, California, come to these clubs. The pay is good, too—more than three times what we make in Suwon."

"No." Hye-yang shook her head emphatically as they boarded the ferry. She thought of the man, his slick mustache, his tobacco breath, the way he slid the pink card into her clothes, her small bag of abalone crashing to the ground. "No, the Folk Village is a good place to work. The best place."

"They have shiny costumes there, and colored lights . . ." Sun pushed her way through the crowd to get them a seat at the front of the boat.

"I'm staying in Suwon," Hye-yang said. "You should, too. Everything we need is there."

"Suit yourself." Sun's hair fluttered back in the breeze as the boat began to move. "But I'm going. We live in the past in Suwon, Hye-yang. I want a future for myself. Think about it. Record players! Fancy makeup! Hair spray! Maybe even a paper star on our door! Some rich American movie man may fall in love with me, take me to Hollywood, California, yes?"

Hye-yang closed her eyes. The salt air entered her pores, sour as the scent of the man's semen. She felt herself swim in a million directions inside, like a sea full of fish.

John James Audubon: The Passenger Pigeon (extinct now)

Everything proved to me that the number of birds resorting to this part of the forest must be immense beyond conception. As the period of their arrival approached, their foes anxiously prepared to receive them. Some were furnished with iron-pots containing sulphur, other with torches of pine-knots, many with poles, and the rest with guns. The sun was lost to our view, yet not a Pigeon had arrived. Every thing was ready, and all eyes were gazing on the clear sky, which appeared in glimpses amidst the tall trees. Suddenly there burst forth a general cry of "Here they come!" The noise which they made, though yet distant, reminded me of a hard gale at sea, passing through the rigging of a close-reefed vessel. As the birds arrived and passed over me, I felt a current of air that surprised me. Thousands were soon knocked down by the pole-men. The birds continued to pour in. The fires were lighted, and a magnificent, as well as wonderful and almost terrifying sight presented itself. The Pigeons, arriving by thousands, alighted everywhere, one above another, until solid masses were formed on the branches all round. Here and there the perches gave way under the weight with a crash, and, falling to the ground, destroyed hundreds of the birds beneath, *forcing down the dense groups with which every stick was loaded. It was a scene of uproar and confusion. I found it quite useless to speak, or even to shout to those persons who were nearest to me. Even the reports of the guns were seldom heard, and I was made aware of the firing only by seeing the shooters reloading.*

No one dared venture within the line of devastation. The hogs had been penned up in due time, the picking up of the dead and wounded being left for the next morning's employment. The Pigeons were constantly coming, and it was past midnight before I perceived a decrease in the number of those that arrived. The uproar continued the whole night; and as I was anxious to know to what distance the sound reached, I sent off a man, accustomed to perambulate the forest, who, returning, two hours afterwards, informed me he had heard it distinctly, when three miles distant from the spot. Towards the approach of day, the noise in some measure subsided: long before objects were distinguishable, the Pigeons began to move off in a direction quite different from that in which they had arrived the evening before, and at sunrise all that were able to fly had disappeared. The howlings of the wolves now reached our ears, and the foxes, lynxes, cougars, bears, raccoons, opossums and pole-cats were seen sneaking off, whilst eagles and hawks of different species, accompanied by a crowd of vultures, came to supplant them, and enjoy their share of the spoil.

*   *   *

It was then that the authors of this devastation began their entry amongst the dead, the dying, and the mangled. The Pigeons were picked up and piled in heaps, until each had as many as he could possibly dispose of, when the hogs were let loose to feed on the remainder.

From the couch, I watch the wind whip across the water. It's already eleven. I must have dozed off again. I've had a headache off and on for a couple of days; Darryl told me to take a day or two off to relax. I admit—it feels nice not to have a bag full of birds in my hand, nice to have such free, empty palms, such light biceps. My headache has already dwindled considerably. A day off is probably just what I needed.

On my way to the Aloha Room for some breakfast, I see a girl—seven, maybe eight years old—building a sand castle on the barnacle-strewn shore. Thick, straight bangs shadow her Coke-bottle glasses, her tea-colored face. She wears a brightly colored, ill-fitting bathing suit with a ridiculous little flounce of skirt in the back. Her legs splay out at strange angles, the skin withered looking, unused. A couple of battered metal canes with arm braces lie on the ground beside her, one on top of the other, like an X.

I realize I haven't seen any children since I arrived at the Salton Sea. It seems strange—wrong, somehow—to see a child here, in this desolate landscape.

The girl continues to pat the mound in front of her. As I get closer, I see it is spiraled with little bits of different plants—drooping marigold, a strip of dyeweed, some ghost flower petals, desert velvet. Her brow is wrinkled in concentration. A putty-colored hearing aid sits in her ear.

The girl looks up, startled. Her glasses make her eyes look extra big, slightly lopsided themselves, the frames askew on her small nose.

"Sorry to bother you," I tell her. "That's quite a castle."

"It's a burial mound," she says, her voice high in her soft palate.

I look more closely at the heap of sand and barnacles and shreds of plant. Something sharp pokes out—the end of a beak. On the other side, the corner of a wing juts through, the feathers dusted with sand. A few other feathers push to the surface around the pile.

"I think maybe this is how the Cahuilla buried people, but maybe I made it up," says the girl.

"You shouldn't be touching these birds." A shiver runs through me. "They have all sorts of awful germs."

"I know." The girl rolls her eyes. "I'll wash my hands as soon as I'm done."

"Is your mother around?" Who would leave their child alone with dead birds? In a bathing suit when the water is contaminated?

"She's in the Aloha," she says. "She said she'd come get me in a little bit."

I suddenly remember being left alone on the beach when I was a girl, a bag of lobsters squirming around by my feet, the claws nudging my skin.

"Are you going to be all right?" I ask her.

"I'm fine." She pats down another plant.

"Don't touch any more birds, please." My headache comes back, a strong pinch between my eyebrows.

She crosses her heart with one slightly shaky finger and goes back to her work.

After I walk into the dark restaurant, I go straight to the bathroom and wash my hands for a long time. I splash some water on my face before I go to the counter.

"There's a little girl playing outside with a dead bird," I tell

Frieda. I can see her through the window, putting something on top of the mound.

"Oh, that's Jeniece," Frieda says. "I've been keeping an eye on her through the glass as best I can. I didn't notice she had a dead bird, though. Damn."

"You know her?"

"Of course I know her, you goofball." She hits me on top of the head with a laminated menu. "She's my daughter!"

"Oh." I fiddle with the napkin dispenser, trying not to flush. "I didn't know you had kids, Frieda."

"Just the one," she says. "My mom usually watches her when I'm at work, but she had a doctor's appointment today. I didn't want her bringing Jeniece to the clinic—Jeniece spends enough time there as it is, and there's all those germs . . ." She looks out the window at her daughter playing with a botulism-infected pelican.

"I better go." She wipes her hands on the apron and rushes outside.

I watch her run to Jeniece. I watch her put her hands on her hips and yell. I watch her turn and walk back to the restaurant. I watch Jeniece stand up and follow after her mother, her metal canes clunking against the barnacles, kicking up dust, her legs dragging behind her as she struggles to catch up.

As soon as they get inside, Frieda points to the bathroom and the girl shuffles off to wash her hands.

"Hi, Ray," Jeniece mumbles as she passes the counter.

"Hey, darlin'." Ray lifts a spatula like a peace sign.

"She was playing with a dead bird!" says Frieda, exasperated.

"She's just a kid, Frieda." Ray goes back to his frying.

Frieda sighs and sits down in the booth across from me. "Ray's so patient," she says. "We got together when Jeniece was three, and from the start, it was like she was his kid more than mine. I mean, of course she's my daughter, of course I love her and everything, but she was just so sick when she was a baby, I didn't want . . ."

"Babe." Ray gestures to Jeniece, who is coming out of the bathroom.

"Hey, kiddo." Frieda raises her voice a notch so that Jeniece can hear her. "Did you wash your hands long enough? The whole ABC song?"

Jeniece shuffles over to a stool at the counter. "'Next time won't you sing with me.'" She rolls her eyes.

On my way home, I stop in front of Jeniece's burial mound. I know I should dig the bird out, bring it back to the hospital, but I can't bear the thought of destroying the girl's intricate decorative work. It almost reminds me of one of my mother's carved eggs, so painstakingly rendered. I replace a bit of desert velvet that has fallen out of place and start to walk back to the trailer.

Wind sweeps across the sea as I walk down Bombay Beach. Dead fish shuttle to the shore by the bucketful. I hold my breath and remember how, when I was around Jeniece's age, my mother and I often went to Casa Cove so that she could skin-dive for lobster.

My mother wore an Esther Williams–style suit, cut low on the hip, bandeau-halter-style on top. I thought she looked like a movie goddess as she came out of the sea, her hair dripping wet over her face, a laundry bag of lobsters hanging by her side. I would hand her a towel; she briskly rubbed it over herself before the lobsters could claw their way out of the bag. She held the towel out, and I draped it back over my shoulder. She walked to the car; I trailed wordlessly behind.

One day, an old surfer—grizzled beard, big tan belly—came up to us as we climbed the sandy slope to the parking lot.

"You skin-dive?" he asked my mother offhandedly, gesturing to the lobster bag at her thighs.

"Forty dollar," she said, her voice suddenly hard, businesslike.

The man looked at her quizzically.

"You make a date later, one hundred dollar," she told him.

"Whoa, lady, I'm not asking you for a date," he said, "I just saw you diving without a tank, and—"

"You dive my skin, one hundred dollar," she repeated.

The man shook his head and walked toward the water. My mother didn't talk at all the whole way home. I leaned my head against the window and drummed on the loose door of the glove cabinet, my thumps punctuated by castanet clicks from the lobster bag.

The next time we went to the beach, we ran into the same guy. He said something to my mother about reconsidering her offer. After she caught her lobsters and a tangle of deep-green kelp, she told me to keep playing. She had somewhere to go.

I watched her climb up the hill in her wet swimsuit flecked with sand. I watched her flick a stray piece of seaweed from her shoulder and yank the suit higher up her hip before she disappeared into a Winnebago parked by a date palm. I saw the man's hairy face flash briefly in the doorway before the door clicked shut. The top of his RV was covered with seagulls.

When my mother came back, she was wearing a blue terry cloth robe I had never seen before. Her swimsuit dangled limp from her wrist, like a purse. Her breath had a weird fruity smell, and she wavered a little bit when she walked. When we drove home, the robe slipped aside and one of her breasts drooped out. Her nipple was the same color as my knee. It was the first time I saw myself reflected in her body.

* * *

That night, I try to call my mother again.

On the answering machine this time, the parrot voice says *"Chal chinaesumnida."* "I am fine."

"I'm glad to hear it, Omma," I say into the phone, "but are you there? Hello? Are you ever going to pick up when I call?"

I wait, but no one answers. I hang up the phone and flop onto the nubby couch. Maybe my mother doesn't want to talk to me until I've saved at least one bird. Maybe she doesn't know what to say. Maybe she just wants to keep the house silent. Maybe she's too depressed to talk to anyone.

Jeniece flashes into my mind but I will her back out. I grab my *chang'go* and slap out a few rhythms. My pulse surges thick in my ears, my headache thick in my brow; I set the drum back down and close my eyes. *No thought, no thought, no thought, no thought.* I follow the slowing beat of my heart, the rise and fall of my own breath, until the waves finally swell and drag me under.

The flowered suitcase in Sun's hand repeatedly banged into Hye-yang's knee as they walked together to the bus station. Hye-yang struggled to keep up with her friend, who walked with quick, eager steps. Sun had just given her notice at the Folk Village. She couldn't stop talking about the outfits she knew would be waiting for her in Kunsan, dresses full of spangles and sequins designed to catch the light. Clothes that sparkle like stars. Clothes that turn girls into stars.

Hye-yang's skull felt stuffed with dirty rags. She couldn't pull together enough clear, clean words to answer her friend. She couldn't move out of the way to avoid the drumbeat smack of the suitcase.

Sun spun around and gave Hye-yang a quick kiss on the lips.

"You're sure you won't come with me?" she asked. She wore sunglasses, a scarf poofed over her hair. Hye-yang turned so that Sun wouldn't see the tears that stung her eyes. When she looked back, Sun had already boarded the bus. She blew a big, stagy kiss from the closing door as the driver pulled away from the curb. Hye-yang watched Sun make her way toward the seats in back, watched her flutter a garish pink handkerchief through an open window until the bus disappeared from view.

Without Sun around, Hye-yang fell into a depression. Her hip hadn't healed completely, and she wasn't able to assume the cor rect archery stance. She could still feel the dock man's body, its squishy heft, in her hand. Her palm felt dirty—she clenched and opened her fist over and over, but she couldn't shake the man off. Her arrows missed the rice straw target, one wayward fling after another.

During the farmer's dance troupe performances, Hye-yang sang so quietly, no one could hear her voice over the drums. In the middle of the *pansori*, she burst into such violent tears that she couldn't continue the song. When she wasn't working, she wouldn't leave her room. Within a month, she was asked to leave the Folk Village.

Hye-yang packed and vacated the room she used to share with Sun, rolling up the sleeping mat that still held some of their twisted-together hair. She walked across the village for the last time and set down her bow and bag of clothes by a pay phone near the cuttlefish stand where she used to work. Trembling, she dialed the number she had copied down at her family's house. Her mother answered after one ring.

"Omma?" Hye-yang asked, her hands, her voice shaking.

"Who is this?" The voice was sharp, clipped.

"It's Hye-yang, Omma. I'm calling you from Suwon."

Hye-yang could hear her mother hold her breath.

"It's your daughter, Omma. It's me, your daughter, Hye-yang." Hye-yang bit her lip.

"My daughter drowned in a diving accident," Hye-yang's mother said before she hung up the phone.

Hye-yang slid to the dirt, cradling the receiver until it pulled from her grasp like an arrow from her bow. The phone swung against a pole, then shot back precariously close to her head. It swayed around for a while before it dangled limp, squawking in Hye-yang's ear.

The dead, fishy scent from the stand overwhelmed Hye-yang.

She wondered if maybe she really had drowned in the ocean, if her body was undulating somewhere underwater, tangled in kelp, gulls swooping down to scoop chunks of her skin into their beaks. Maybe she was a ghost; maybe she had been one even before she left Cheju-do the first time. Maybe the man on the beach with the shiny suit had only wanted to show her the way to the afterlife, show her where she needed to go.

Fighting nausea, Hye-yang stood slowly and hung up the phone. She hesitated for a moment before she pulled a pink business card, the one Sun had given her, out of the folds of her jacket. Her fingers felt cold, waterlogged, heavy with the dock man's flesh, as she lifted the receiver again.

I wake before the sun rises. My headache seems better, just the faint ghost of a throb. I turn on the air conditioner, bow to the cool rush of air, and begin to practice some of my *hyung*s before it gets too hot. The trailer is too small for all my favorite kicks, all my thrusts of arm and heel, but there is enough space for a small repertoire. The first couple of times I practiced tae kwon do in the trailer, I worried I might rock it right off its platform, but now I feel slightly more steady, slightly more rooted this high in the air.

I bow once again to the AC, then sit on the bed and listen to my heart pound. I tell myself it's because of my vigorous blocking moves and not the fact that I'm going to see Darryl soon. I'm surprised by how excited I am to get back to work, dismal as the work itself may be.

I decide to walk to the bird hospital. It's not too hot this early in the day, and I can always get a ride later if I don't want to walk home. I grab some extra bags and rubber gloves before I leave, in case I find a bird or two along the way.

A diffuse light teases the sky as I climb down the ladder. The pigeons are already awake in the rusted-out, half-drowned trailers on the other side of the berm. They fly in and out of the windows with rushing gurgles of throat, sharp ruffles of wing. I wish them well as I step down to the rung where they disappear from view.

My feet register the place where the asphalt turns to barnacle. The Aloha and its parking lot stand silhouetted, still dark in the distance, as I crunch across the beach. More pale light leaks into the air. I see Jeniece's burial mound a couple of yards away. It has been destroyed. The pelican has been dragged away by wild dogs, maybe a coyote. A few bones are scattered about—curve of skull, tip of wing, bits of skin and feather clinging to strewn white shards. The desert plants Jeniece had so carefully arranged are flung all over the barnacles. The site looks like the aftermath of a wild party, or an amateur paleontology dig.

I nudge a bird rib with my shoe. When I was ten, I wanted to be a paleontologist. I thought my future was in dirt, in bones. My class had just finished a unit on dinosaurs, and I was filled with awe. As I had my after-school snack, I told my mother there had been two classes of dinosaurs in the world—bird-hipped dinosaurs and lizard-hipped ones. I told her that birds probably came from the bird-hipped dinosaurs long after they died away.

She grabbed my arms. "What will come after all the birds die?" she asked, her eyes fierce. "You tell me. What will come then?"

A piece of my little walnut-shaped cake caught in my throat.

"Omma," I coughed. I pulled myself away from her grasp, stumbled to the sink, and tilted my head under the faucet. As I looked up at the water, I imagined that's what birds would turn into next—a clear ribbony rush, stippled with light. If something as big as a dinosaur could turn into something as small as a bird, wouldn't that be the next logical step—from scale to feather to pure liquid shimmer? I turned to try to explain this to my mother, but she had already left the room.

I rest my toe in part of the pelican's hip bone. I put my hands on my own hips, feel their contours, the ridges of bone that swell beneath my khaki pants. I have lizard hips, dinosaur hips—so much broader, more earthbound, than my mother's slight bird-hipped frame. I squat down, slip on my rubber gloves, and begin to scoop the bones into a plastic bag. Better for Jeniece to see things flattened down to normal than find her work in such grisly disarray. I smooth out the sand and barnacles with my covered palms.

A small hunk of bird flesh and feathers tumbles away toward the shore; I follow it. The garbage bag feels so light—it's amazing how little the bones weigh. A whole dead pelican in these same bags feels like a stone.

I pick up the piece of bird as the sun lifts over the hills. The air instantly feels about twenty degrees hotter. The sea begins to sparkle like root beer. I wipe away the sweat that pops onto my forehead and notice a shell on the ground up ahead. I haven't seen any like it here before—a pale pink disk among the barnacles. I put the bird remains in the bag and reach for it. It squishes between my gloved fingers, resists when I try to pick it up. I jump back. Some of the surrounding barnacles fall away. The shell is attached to skin. The shell itself *is* skin—a nipple, I realize with a bolt of nausea. A breast. I stumble backward over the bumpy ground, kicking loose more barnacles. A collarbone. A bruised throat. An open mouth, filled with small white shells.

I drop the garbage bag and run to the Aloha Room. I bang on the door, but Frieda and Ray aren't in. I race to the bird hospital. Inside the chain-link enclosure, the temperature rises. Everything seems to spin.

"Ava, hi!"

I can hear Abby, but I can't see her.

"Are you ready to be back yet? It looks like you still have a headache . . ."

I bend over. "A woman." I gasp for air.

"I'm sorry?" Abby asks.

"I thought she was a shell . . ."

"Do you have a fever?" Abby touches my forehead with her gloved hand. "I think she's delirious," I hear her say to someone else.

"Ava, are you okay?" It's Darryl, his voice full of concern.

"I saw a woman." My breath begins to steady. My eyes begin to focus again. Darryl's generous lips, Abby's freckles zoom into sharp relief. "A dead woman on the beach."

"What?" Abby asks, alarmed.

"She was in the barnacles. I thought she was a shell."

"Oh my god," says Darryl. "Ava, are you okay?"

I nod my head, sit down on the dirt floor.

"I'm calling the police," says Abby. "Which beach was it—Bombay?"

I nod again.

"Let me get you some water." Darryl lightly touches my hair.

I dip my head between my knees. My pulse pounds loud in my ears. I flash again on the woman on the beach, the woman with no pulse, no breath. I think of the woman's open mouth; my own tongue fills with chalky barnacle grit.

"Here you go." Darryl holds a water bottle out to me. I sit up and take a long, grateful swallow.

"The police are on their way," Abby says. "Did it look like heat stroke or something?"

I shake my head. "She was naked. Someone tried to bury her . . ." The room begins to spin again.

"Annyong hasnimnikka?" is on the tape when I call home a few hours later—Kane's voice, from the recording I had given my mother after he died.

"No, Omma, no, I'm not exactly at peace," I say into the yeasty-smelling receiver. "I found a body today. A dead woman. Murdered." I close my eyes. I'm sure I can feel every corpuscle that scuttles through my veins. "I don't know what I'm doing, Omma. I don't know what I'm doing here anymore. Maybe I should come home . . ." The machine cuts me off.

A while later, I try again.

"Tell them you know the language of birds," my mother's

voice, her real voice, crackles on the answering machine tape—a command, not a suggestion. My heart flip-flops at the sound of it. I wait for more, but there is just the sizzle of static, then the beep.

"Omma," I say into the phone. "If I knew the language of birds, I probably wouldn't be here in the first place. Are you there? Why won't you talk with me? Omma? Hello?"

The machine beeps, cutting me off again. I press redial and listen to my mother's voice one more time, but I can't think of anything else to say.

It is only later, as I'm trying to sleep, that I remember the folktale my mother used to tell me, the one about the two brothers who knew the language of birds.

One day these brothers were walking down the street when a crow let out a plaintive caw. From this, they knew a man was being stabbed a couple of blocks away. They ran to the scene of the crime to see if they could help and found the man splayed in a pool of blood. One brother put his head to the man's chest to try to detect a heartbeat; the other put his hand over the man's nose and mouth to see if he could feel any breath. The police arrived, and seeing the brothers kneeling over the body, their hands covered with blood, they immediately charged them with murder.

At their trial, the brothers tried to explain what had happened. They told the judge about the crow, his message; they told about their attempt to help. "So you know the language of birds," the judge sneered. "Tell me, then, what the crane perched in the persimmon tree outside is carrying on about!"

The brothers looked at the bird through the window and listened intently. They turned to face each other, unsure of how to proceed. One brother flushed and cleared his throat.

"Your Honor," he stammered, "the bird says, 'Please return my eggs to me, the ones you have hidden inside your sleeve.'"

The brothers grasped each other's hands. They knew they could be sent to their deaths, saying such a thing to a judge. The guards rushed toward them, but the judge held up his palm. He rolled back the long sleeve of his *chogori;* three eggs balanced there inside the crook of his elbow. The crane beat its wings wildly. A shower of persimmons fell from the tree. The judge let the brothers go.

My mother must think I will be accused of this murder. The police did question me a long time, much longer than necessary, it seemed, but they let me go with nothing more ominous than a snide thank-you, a slightly leering "we'll be in *touch*." They had asked all sorts of personal questions—questions about my sexual preference, my sexual history (when I said "none to speak of," they just laughed in my face). They asked if I was a U.S. citizen, they asked if I was born in this country; they asked my reasons for being in the area; they wanted to know everything I've done here, everyone I've talked to. They asked me why I had touched the victim—specifically why I had touched her nipple, why I had gloves on my hands. They asked if I had touched her genitals. They asked if I had touched her neck, if I had kissed her. They asked if I liked it rough. They asked questions until I was shaking so hard, I thought my skull would vibrate right through my scalp. I doubt it would have helped much had I told them I know the language of birds.

Hye-yang looked through the window as the bus to Kunsan cut through acre upon acre of rice paddies. Rows of slender green plants spread out in all directions, as far as she could see. The shoots, hip-high, were tinged a brassy blonde, almost pinkish, in the sunset; the bus exhaust parted some of them, revealing their dark-green roots, the damp scalp of earth underneath. Hye-yang watched white ducks walk between the rows, dipping their beaks into narrow furrows of water, tilting their heads back to swallow.

A few olive military vehicles passed the bus. Hye-yang leaned off her seat and watched the fortified camp town come into view through the windshield. The bus pulled up to the gate and stopped. Hye-yang made her way to the front, hesitated near the driver for a moment, then stepped out into the dusty air. The stone wall that surrounded the town cast a broad shadow across her face.

She started to walk through the gates, when a U.S. Air Force guard put his hand flat on her breastbone to stop her.

"Excuse me, Miss? Your registration card?"

Hye-yang stared at him.

"You can't come in without your card." He left his hand there.

Hye-yang looked back at the bus. She had the urge to jump back on, to go back to Suwon, but it began to pull away, spewing a cloud of exhaust in her direction.

"All the girls need their cards," the guard said, slowly this time.

"Card?" Hye-yang pulled the pink card out from her jacket and showed it to him. "I come sing here," she said.

"Oh, a new girl." He looked her up and down with a sly smile that reminded her of the dock man, then let his hand trail down the front of her shirt before he pointed her through the gates.

Hye-yang felt disoriented as she entered the camp town. The dusty road, lined with shops and clubs, was busy, but not in the same way the Folk Village had been. Even the weekend crowds there had felt polite, friendly. This was a frantic busy. A dark, noisy, careless busy. American men, some in uniform, some not, barreled up to her, one after another, speaking too fast for her to understand, putting their hands on her body as she rushed by. Small children, some strangely pale, others strangely dark, played unsupervised, barely clothed, in the street. Neon lights began to sputter on over the clubs, spelling out words she could barely understand—SHANGRI-LALA, SEXXY GIRL, PASTIES PLACE. She finally spotted the hissing sign that carried the name she recognized from the business card—WILD TING. Under the yellow letters, an orange neon woman jerkily shook her hips from side to side, a pink tail sprouting from her bikini bottoms. The light that formed her face was burnt out, the tubes dark, dirty looking.

Hye-yang pushed her way inside the dim, smoky club. The air was filled with the sweet stench of rotten fruit. A woman's shrill, false laughter rang out over the flat din of voices, the tinny jukebox music. Glancing over the heads of dark-skinned military men and the women who leaned toward them, Hye-yang caught a glimpse of Sun, standing on top of the bar. As she pushed through the crowd toward her friend, she felt a rush of relief, of happiness, wash over her.

"Sun!" she yelled. "Sun!" She remembered seeing Sun at the Folk Village for the first time, Sun the bride, with pink cheeks and flowers in her hair. She remembered the way Sun's face broke into joy when she saw Hye-yang in the crowd. Hye-yang edged her way closer to the bar. She called Sun's name again, but her friend didn't look her way. She looked like she couldn't see anything, like she was looking at something far beyond the walls of the club. Her hair was frizzed out, a big puffball around her head.

"Sun!" she yelled, frantically this time. She began to wonder if she was indeed a ghost, if her edges had already started to disappear.

As Hye-yang pushed her way through to the bar stools, she realized with a shock that Sun was wearing nothing but a T-shirt, not even panties. She watched, stunned, as Sun squatted down and lifted a coin from the sticky wood veneer of the bar with her vagina. Sun wiggled around, then dropped the coin into the waiting mouth of a GI who stared at her from a red bar stool, running a hand up her bare leg. Hye-yang turned her head. She had never seen Sun's naked body before, had never seen any woman's naked body before, not even her own, not between the legs. When she and Sun shared a room at the Folk Village, they always changed behind screens, never showing each other anything. Hye-yang wondered if her own body looked so purplish down there, so wrinkled and tired.

"Sun," Hye-yang said again. The name sounded like a sob.

Sun looked down.

"Hye-yang," she said dreamily. She bent down so her crotch was right in Hye-yang's face. A strong smell wafted out, like cuttle-fish. Hye-yang suppressed a gag. Sun reached out and touched Hye-yang's face. The man who had taken the coin in his mouth put his hand on Hye-yang's hip.

Hye-yang pulled away and pushed back through the crowded bar, back out into the dusty air. She collapsed against the side of the building and tried to take a deep breath.

"Are you okay?" A man with dark skin crouched down beside her.

She looked up. "My friend," she started, not sure what to say in English.

"You work with your friend?" He licked his upper lip and smiled.

"At Folk Village," she said, glad to have someone to talk to, someone with kind eyes.

He nodded.

"In Suwon," she said.

"Your friend's named Sue?"

"Sun. In Suwon."

"Soon, hell yeah—in Sue, on Sue, anytime sounds good to me. How much?"

"I know her since little girl."

"Just like sisters. Damn! What's the damage?"

Sun sidled up next to Hye-yang. "Fifty, for both," she said, then put her arms around Hye-yang and kissed her. Hye-yang felt Sun's thick tongue in her mouth and jumped back. She was glad to see Sun had put on a skirt, even though it barely covered her hips.

"That sounds more than reasonable. Fuck Village. Damn!" He tapped the wallet in the back of his pants, then put one arm around Hye-yang, one around Sun. Hye-yang resisted as he tried to pull her away from the wall.

"Come on, baby," he said, his lips against her ear.

"Come on, Hye-yang," Sun said, then glanced back nervously at the front door of the bar. "I be with you."

Hye-yang didn't budge.

A familiar-looking man with a thin mustache and a shiny suit burst out of Wild Ting.

"Sun! Where are you going?" he yelled.

"My friend is here," she said. "My friend come to visit me!"

"You are still on my clock." He glared at her. "You make sure you bring me my cut."

Sun flipped her middle finger at him, then tugged at Hye-yang. Hye-yang couldn't move. She wanted to tell Sun about the man at the dock, but it was like the man's hand was still clamped over her mouth, shoving her voice somewhere deep inside, somewhere she couldn't access. She wanted to tell Sun about her phone call with her mother; she almost wanted to believe her mother's story.

I am floating in the ocean, she thought as the man stormed toward them. *I had a diving accident and now I'm a ghost. I'm covered with kelp. Birds are tearing me apart. He's here to show me where to go.*

Albino Cockatiel, Name: Man Jang.

Ava, daughter, age 14,
see bird look at self in window.
She find Sun's old face make up
under my bed, put in birdcage,
circle open like a shell.
He love mirror inside,
bob head up and down,
watch white feathers
flick and spread on top.
Next day he tip over, pink dust
all over cheek. Maybe he try
to eat powder and choke.
Maybe sun hit mirror
and burn him with too much light.

5/17/85

I don't know where I should be right now. Part of me wants to go back to San Diego. Being here is ridiculous—so much death. The woman, the birds. The birds I haven't helped yet. And how can I go back to San Diego if I haven't helped the birds? And how can I stay here, walking around by myself on the beach, knowing some murderer is out there? Darryl probably has people teaming up now. He probably won't let anyone go out on their own. Maybe he'd volunteer to come with me on my rounds . . .

I want to see what's going on at the hospital, but I can't seem to get out of bed. I can't seem to answer the phone, even though it rings several times, even though I know it may finally be my mother, finally calling me back. Frieda eventually comes over to check on me.

"It's a shame, what happened to that girl." She puts a Tupperware batch of chicken and rice soup in the fridge for me to microwave later. Her hands still smell of broth when she comes over to the bed.

"And, Ava." Frieda's breath smells of broth, too; it wafts over me like a chicken-scented humidifier. "It's a shame you had to find her, but life goes on, honey . . ."

I bury my head beneath the pillow. Frieda pulls it off.

"We're all scared, Ava, all of us. There's still a killer out there somewhere. Emily's gone near out of her mind with fear, and what's that gonna do for us? Nothing. Nothing! Lying around feeling sorry for yourself isn't gonna help that girl you found none. She's gone. We here gotta keep on living, even with some maniac running around. So stop feeling sorry for yourself and get out of that bed!" Frieda slaps a hand against my blanketed thigh.

I keep my eyes closed as my body gently rocks on the bed from the reverberation of Frieda's slap. I don't think it's myself I'm feeling sorry for. I think of my mother, the blank look on her face when she read about the prostitute killed in Korea. I remember the way she closed her bedroom door behind her.

"Ava, open your eyes." Frieda shakes me by the arms, but I can barely feel it. "Snap out of it! We need your help."

I let my eyelids slide open; they feel like they are about a mile long the way they drag over my irises.

"What kind of help could I possibly give you?" I ask Frieda before I flip onto my stomach. So far I've only helped the statistics people, the cleanup people. I exhale loudly into the musty sheets.

"You know that kung fu stuff, right?" Frieda asks. I roll back over and sit up. Frieda cocks a knowing, penciled-on eyebrow.

Now, every Tuesday and Thursday morning in the Aloha Room after the regular breakfast crowd leaves, I find myself teaching tae kwon do lessons for women. At around ten, Frieda shoos Ray out of the restaurant and puts a cardboard sign on the door that says CLOSED FOR SELF-DEFENSE PURPOSES, under which Emily has scrawled "Yea, we girls are gonna kick your butt!" Someone else has crossed out "girls" and written "WOMEN!" over it with a green pen.

The regular group, besides Frieda and Emily, consists of four women in their sixties—Betty, Pat, Myrna, and Sue, who normally play bridge those mornings but decided to try something new; Lonnie, a gravelly-voiced park ranger; and Rayanne, who owns the Pretty Poodle grooming shop in Salton City and looks a bit like a poodle herself.

I have never taught a self-defense class before. I have never *taken* a strictly self-defense class before, just the straight martial art. I hope the women in her class can't sense how lost I feel.

I start each session with a formal bow, just as all of my tae kwon do classes have begun. The bowing atmosphere in the Aloha Room is vastly different from that at the *dojang*. I remember how solemn the bows had felt there, how quiet, and almost sacred. Here, the bowing is accompanied by a bunch of groans and "Oh, my back!'s," plus pseudo-Asian voices saying "Ah so," and variations on "Confucius say bend over." I consider scrapping the whole bowing thing but can't bring myself to do it. I bow even when I practice by myself.

The bridge ladies, in their soft pastel jogging suits, are surprisingly intense once it comes time to do the *hyung*s, the forms. I would not want to be cornered by them in a dark alley. Frieda, still wearing her Hawaiian shirt, is amazingly focused, too, although her blocks and punches lack a lot of oomph; she looks more like she is dancing than learning how to protect herself. Emily spends much of the time with her hands on her hips, exasperated, which is strange, since she is a tap dancer and must be at least somewhat coordinated. Short, stocky, windburned, Lonnie is almost frightening in her ferocity; she lets out harsh yells with every kick and punch, like someone from a Godzilla movie, if not the monster itself. Rayanne looks near tears half the time and approaches each new form with timid hands and feet, a poodle trying to avoid a puddle.

"So when are we gonna start the *fighting?*" Frieda asks one Thursday morning, after an hour of *hyung*s. "We've just been kicking the air . . ."

"Yeah, we could beat up a light breeze just fine, is about it," adds Emily, who hasn't even been beating up the air very much.

"I wanna feel some *booty* under my foot!" Frieda slaps Emily's hand.

"Sparring is kind of tricky," I hesitate. "You have to be really careful not to hurt the other person. It takes a while to learn the kind of control you need—you have to use full power, but deflect it, not use it on the other person, pull away before you hit."

"Kind of like Rick," says Emily. "He needs to work on that—he always says he's gonna pull out in time, but sometimes he just can't control himself, you know how he is. It's a good thing I can clench myself up tight in there, so those sperms of his don't get through."

"Clenching isn't gonna stop any babies from starting, sweetie pie," Frieda says. "You need to get that boy some condoms."

"Do you mind?" Rayanne blanches, puts a thin hand over her pursed mouth.

"Well, this *is* a *protection* class, is it not?" Frieda demands. "We gals gotta look out for each other."

"Besides." I clear my throat, try to veer the conversation back into its original direction. "We need some mats. This floor is too hard for sparring."

"I know a gym teacher down at the high school in Indio," says Lonnie. "I'm sure we could drag some mats over here, no problem."

"You look into that," I tell her, "but we still need to work on our forms some more before we start getting at it."

There is a collective groan.

"This is important. We don't want to hurt each other, right?"

"Couldn't we get one of those guys that dress up in big foam suits with a big foam head and everything and you can just pummel away at 'em and they don't feel a thing?" Frieda asks. "I saw one on a rerun. *Roseanne,* I think."

"Yeah," a few other voices murmur. The bridge ladies nod in assent.

"I don't know where we'd find a costume like that," I say.

"Well, I volunteer Rick, costume or no," says Emily.

Frieda slaps Emily's hand again, then looks at her watch.

"Okay, girls," she says, "time to clear out. I gotta start the lunch stuff."

The crowd of women suddenly disperse, like a drop of dye spattered onto water.

"Hey," I call out, "we haven't done our closing bow!" But no one hears me. The bridge ladies are already out the door, and Lonnie and Rayanne are struggling with their shoes. Frieda and Emily have disappeared into the kitchen. As the grill hisses on, sending the hot smell of grease into the air, I bow to the plastic hula woman who swivels from the ceiling, slightly deflated, her left foot almost flat as she bows subtly back.

A couple of nights later, Emily and Frieda invite me to join them for cards at Emily's place. I'm not much of a card person—my mother often played the flower card game, just never with me—but I say yes, if only to avoid another nervous evening alone in the trailer. I'm surprised by how nice it is to spend time with other people, surprised by how sad I was when I found out that Abby went back to Colorado shortly after the body was found. I've never been much of a people person before. Maybe the birds are shoving me into human company.

At the faux-wood laminated table, Emily is holding an open package of ramen. She crunches a corner of stiff, pale noodles off the folded block, still in their cellophane wrapper. The foil flavor packet peeks precariously out of the corner. Either it will fall or Emily will bite into it by accident and get a mouth full of monosodium glutamate.

"I didn't know you could eat ramen raw," I tell her.

"It's not *raw*, exactly." Emily's teeth pass through the noodles with a sound I wish I could sample. It could be used for part of an iceberg breaking off, or someone walking on leaves. I have to remember to carry my little recorder with me at all times. "It's already fried and everything. It's just faster this way."

"Ramen only takes three minutes to cook, Emily." Frieda shakes her head as she shuffles the deck of cards.

"I just like it, okay?" Emily crumbles off a chunk of noodle, holds out her hand to offer it to anyone. Frieda and I decline. "Plus they're cheap—eleven cents a pop, cheaper than those chow mein noodles, and it's pretty much the same thing. So deal already."

"I don't know if I can," says Frieda.

"You don't know if you can what?" Emily washes the dry noodles down with a swig from her bottle of peach wine cooler.

"Deal with your ramen-eating shenanigans." Frieda sounds
mournful.

"Deal the *cards,* you idiot!" Emily sits down. A spray of hard
white crumbs land on the table in front of her as she rubs her
hands together. "I wanna take you girls for all I can get."

I wonder how many packets of ramen noodles I have con-
sumed in my lifetime. They were a staple in my house growing
up—sometimes my mother and I had them for dinner every night
of the week, sometimes with a bit of Buddig's paper-thin lunch-
meat turkey, the cheapest meat we could find, sliced in. This was
usually after there had been a sting at the massage parlor where
my mother worked, when she went for weeks without pay before
the business opened up again in another location. When I was ten,
she stayed in jail for two days after one of those stings. I pooled all
of my change together and bought eight packs of ramen at Lucky's
so that I would have something to eat until she came home. I avoid
ramen whenever possible now.

Frieda dusts some of the crumbles off the scratched-up table
and dives into the card game with a fierceness I have not seen in
her before, certainly not in self-defense class. I have trouble focus-
ing on the cards—the smell of the noodles between Emily's teeth is
too distracting—and I'm quickly out, owing three dollars.

I drift away from the table, leaving Emily and Frieda to battle
to the death themselves. I look at the knickknacks in the china
cabinet—Precious Times figurines, little blonde angel babies—the
dusty silk flowers, the Miss Tomato ribbon, a Kmart portrait of
Emily with her boyfriend, his hand up her shirt.

I step outside. The sky is clear, the smog swept away by a
warm breeze that makes the palm trees sway gently. They look
like women dancing while they do the dishes—humming a little

tune, not performing, not even aware they are moving, just following the music in their heads, their hands full of suds. A few
orangey dates, too small to eat, are strewn about on the ground. I
roll one around with the toe of my sandal. Somewhere a bird calls
out, a sweet, healthy cry, and I try to telepathically tell it to fly
away, get out of here; this place won't support your song.

"It's *hot* out here." Emily steps outside. She lifts her arms over
her head, as if to take the heat in, and I catch a whiff of her
deodorant and the sweat it isn't entirely preventing. Emily wiggles
around a bit, like the palm trees, but I can tell Emily is conscious
of her own little dance. Emily is used to being watched, and she
moves accordingly, sashaying her hips from side to side as she
climbs a few stairs when a man is behind her, throwing her head
back to laugh when some guy tells a joke, bending her leg up onto
the chair, so whoever it is can get a peek of her panties. She holds
a wine cooler out to me, and I take it hesitantly, twist off the top. It
is sickeningly sweet, but it is cold.

"Where's Frieda?" I pick at the label on the bottle.

"She's cleaning up."

"You let Frieda clean up your house?"

Emily takes a swig. "I sure as hell don't like to do it."

We sit down on the small concrete platform by the front door.

"The stars are amazing tonight." I look at my bottle. The wine
looks like it is glowing inside, radioactive, the way Emily's porch
lantern shines through it. The bubbles stream up like shooting stars.

"That's Cassiopeia up there," Emily points out. "And Cygnus,
the swan."

I look up and lift my bottle to the sky, sending a toast to all the
swans in Estonia. I wonder how they are doing—the news never
followed up on the story, and the Estonian consulate never
answered my letter. I hope they are faring better than my poor
pelicans.

"Plus the dippers are out, Ursa Major and Minor." Emily's hot pink fingernail skitters around more. "And Draco's right there, too."

"How do you know so much about stars?" I ask.

"Well, actually . . ." Emily arches her back to see the sky better, and probably to stick up her breasts, although if it is for my benefit, it isn't working. All it does is show me the line of sweat beneath them on Emily's neon-green tank top. "I don't know if I told you how I lived in San Bernardino for a while?"

I shake my head.

"I was living with this guy who owned a billiards and bar stools store, Kenny. I worked there part time for a while. My main thing was to wear these little skirts and bend over the pool tables. I sold a lot of pool tables." Emily demonstrates, sticking the back of her white shorts into my face.

"I'll bet." I turn away, swallow down some more of the sweet wine while Emily sits back down.

"Kenny was very into me making something of myself, you know? So I took some classes at the junior college. I signed up for world history or something or other and film appreciation—like you have to go to college to learn how to watch a movie! I flunked out, though. The classes were at the same time as my soaps."

"Hmm." I can feel the alcohol kicking in; I don't drink very often. My shoulder blades tingle.

"Kenny was furious. He said how am I going to be an educated woman if I don't go to class? So I signed up for this class—I thought it was cosmetology, you know, makeup and all that? So I signed up, but when I went to the first class it wasn't about lipstick or hair care or anything!"

"What was it?"

"It was cos*mol*ogy." Emily shakes her head and laughs. "Stars. The universe and shit."

"And you took the class?"

"The teacher was cute. We did it in the planetarium this one time. He put on the stars and everything. It was cool."

"And you learned a lot?"

"I got a B, but that's only because I didn't do the homework. He told me if I was as good a student as I was a lay, he would have given me an A-plus-plus!" Emily lights up a cigarette, obviously pleased with herself.

"What about Kenny?"

"That asshole? I found him doing it on a pool table with this floozy from accounting. She didn't even look good in a short skirt!"

"Well . . ." I don't know what to say.

"So I moved back here. I figured that's all the bettering of myself I needed to do."

"I see . . ."

"So anyway, that's the Corona Borealis." Emily points back up at the stars with her cigarette. The lit end of it whizzes like a comet in front of my face. I wonder if I should ask her about the two constellations that supposedly come together once every summer, the ones from the Korean folktale about the star-crossed lovers who can only see each other when birds form a bridge across the Milky Way.

The screen door suddenly opens against our backs. Emily and I scoot out of the way to let Frieda through.

"Jeez, it's hot out here," she says. "Why don't you girls come back inside?"

"Just what I was thinking." Emily throws her wine-cooler bottle out into the yard. It crashes against something, but Emily doesn't seem to care. She just stubs out her cigarette, and with a swivel of hips she is back inside.

"I think I'm going to head back home." I stand up. "Tell Emily I said thanks for the hospitality."

"Will do, hon." Frieda gives me a little hug. "You be careful now. Keep your keys out in front of you."

"Sure thing. See you tomorrow."

Frieda goes back inside. The screen door clinks behind her.

I look for Emily's bottle so that I can bring it home and put it in my recycling bin along with the bottle I have almost finished myself, but it had shattered in pieces on Emily's green gravel yard. The force of it had taken part of the ear off one of Emily's little gnome statues. I suddenly flash on Jeniece, her hearing aid. She must be with Ray tonight. I wonder what they do together—watch TV, play cards, build burial mounds?

I look up again at the sky, my hands full of glass. I try, and fail, to find the swan again before I get into the car.

The ride home is a bit squirrelly; I try to focus on the road, but I feel like the tires are sliding over ice. By the time I make it back to the trailer, my mouth is completely dry. I pound down a glass of ginger lemonade, then a glass of water, but it doesn't help. My thirst doesn't feel connected to my tongue, the back of my throat; it's a tipsy thirst that shoots through my bones.

I pick up my *chang'go,* and with each thrum of my fingers, each slap from the heel of my palm, I feel drenched in sound, my heart bursting open into a million drops of water. I feel my mind sharpen back into focus.

The phone rings. I tuck the receiver between my shoulder and my ear so that I can continue to play.

"Hello?" I drum softly so that I can hear who called. No one responds.

"Hello?" I drop the drumming down another notch. Still no answer. I am about to hang up when someone clears their throat.

"Hello?" I ask again. "Is someone there?"

Then the person starts to sing.

"Omma?" I whisper.

My mother's voice swirls out of the holes of the receiver, a mournful sound. I close my eyes and begin to play the drum with stronger hands.

Hye-yang quickly learned the way of the *kijich'on*:

- No throwing up inside the club. No throwing up outside the club. No throwing up where the GIs might see you.
- Stay in the DMZ. The Dark Man Zone is where you work. You are a Dark Man girl. Black GIs only. Don't even stick your head in a white man club.
- Bring your money directly back to the bar. You owe the bar for your room and board, your clothes, your television, your radio, all of your cosmetics. You will be paying the bar back for a long time. Don't even think about keeping the money for yourself. Don't even think about trying to escape before you have paid back your debt. They have a peephole into your bedroom. They'll know if you're planning any funny business. They'll always track you down.
- Sell drinks to the GIs. As many drinks as you can. Water them down before you bring them to the table. Get the GIs to buy you drinks. Water those drinks down even more.
- You will choose an American name, one the GIs can say and remember.
- You will keep your ID on you at all times, with the name of this bar on the front, your menstrual calendar on the back. You will go to the VD clinic every week to make sure you

are clean. If you are infected, you will be sent to the Monkey House; this is not something you will enjoy.

~ You will bleed the first time, maybe the first several times. You will hurt for a long time between your legs. Your jaw will ache. You will think you are going to die. You will think that you want to die. Don't worry. Before too long it won't hurt anymore. Before too long, you won't feel anything at all.

~ Your friend will take pills. Lots of little orange pills. It will look like someone has pulled your friend's heart right out of her body. She will float around you like a ghost. She will grab on to you and cry; other times she will pluck at your hair and laugh like a machine gun. She will talk about being a star. She still believes one day she will be a star. She will take little orange pills and drink tall glasses of watered-down vodka. She will tell you stories you won't even want to begin to believe.

Does that girl have a silver face?" Frieda gapes at the teenager walking into the Aloha Room—a surprising sight in itself, silver face or no.

"Either that or I'm hallucinating right along with you, babe." Ray squeezes Frieda's shoulders.

"Maybe there's something in the water today." Emily lifts her eyebrows and holds out her glass for more.

I imagine Emily in her Miss Tomato costume. I imagine a bunch of pelicans hoisting themselves up onto the bar stools. Anything's possible inside these walls.

The girl stops at the hostess stand. She looks like a cartoon, a smiley face smeared with metallic paint, her blonde braids streaked with green. A stretch of skin sparkles between her tank top and flannel rocket-ship pajama bottoms. Just behind her, another girl comes in, sporting tufts of bright-pink hair, a purple sports bra, army pants with a baby-doll face sewn on to each knee. Both girls have about two dozen candy necklaces bunched around their throats. They are smiling, smiling, almost demonically smiling, their teeth a dazzle of orange and blue from the neon by the door.

After being around dead birds all day, I almost can't look at these girls—they seem too full of color, too full of life.

"It's too early for Halloween, isn't it?" Frieda asks.

Ray sings the theme from *The Twilight Zone*—"do do do do"—under his breath.

"What a funky place!" The girl with pink hair looks around the room in awe.

"Yeah," says the girl with the silver face. "It's got that retro tiki thing going." They pounce on each other, rub each other's hair.

"Retro means washed up, right?" Frieda asks, eyes fretful.

"Retro's cool, Frieda," Emily whispers back. "Like old T-Birds and stuff."

"I ain't no old T-Bird, yet," Frieda says. She puts her hands on her hips and glares at the girls.

Silver Face pulls a menu from the stand. "I knew it!" she says. "Check out the 'Diet Plate'!"

Pink Hair reads out loud, "'Ground beef hamburger steak, cottage cheese, peach half, dinner roll.' No way!" The girls laugh so hard, they have to hold each other up.

Frieda sidles out from behind the counter. "Can I help you?" she asks. She looks stung; I know she eats that Diet Plate just about every night.

"Yeah—do you have any vegan chow?" Silver Face asks.

Frieda crosses her arms below her breasts. "Is that like Puppy Chow?" She arches an eyebrow. I've never heard her voice like this before—snide, almost mean. Somehow I get the feeling Jeniece has heard it plenty of times.

The girls laugh even harder. "We don't eat animal products," says Pink Hair.

"We have fried fish," says Frieda, and they fall on the floor laughing, their platform sneakers churning the air. Frieda throws up her hands in exasperation and storms back to the counter.

Silver Face links eyes with me. She stops laughing.

"Oh my gosh," she says. "You are soooo beautiful." She makes a beeline for my stool. My breath catches. She wraps her arms around my shoulders. Her makeup presses damp against my cheek. I can feel the heat of her body pass through my clothes. Pink Hair giggles from the ground. The baby doll's eyes open and close on her knees. I can't move.

"Get off her already," Ray barks after what feels like a year.

Silver Face glides away as if on roller skates.

"Are you okay, Ava?" he asks.

I nod, my nostrils full of her greasepaint-bubble-gum scent, my skin suddenly cool.

Silver Face beams at me. "No one can see how beautiful she is, but I can!"

"Me too," says Pink Hair from the floor. Baby eyes blink, blink in my direction. She blows me a kiss.

Why can't I move?

"Okay," Frieda shouts. "That's enough! You both get out of here right now!"

"But we're hungry," says Pink Hair.

"Eat your goddamn necklaces," says Frieda. "Shoo!"

Silver Face looks straight at me again. "You're beeeeautiful!" she trills. She grabs Pink Hair's hand. A square piece of paper flies out of her back pocket as they fly out the door.

"They're on X," says Emily.

"They're on something, that's for sure," Frieda scoffs.

"Ecstasy, definitely." Emily nods her head. "I did it once. It makes you all huggy and lovey and everything. It makes you want to grab everyone in sight."

"You must have X running through your veins, then, woman." Frieda starts to wipe off the counter.

Emily picks up the piece of paper and snaps it in the air like a flag. "I knew it—they're going to a rave!"

"Around here?" asks Ray.

"On the Indian reservation." Emily scans the flyer. "'Desert Dogma Smash.' We should go!"

"No way," says Frieda. "I'm not hanging around a bunch of whacked-out, technicolor teenagers."

"Oh, come on. It'll be fun. Raves are like outside discos!"

"Have you ever been to one?" Frieda asks.

"No, but . . ."

"We told Jeniece we'd rent a movie tonight," says Ray.

"Frieda, you can blow it off, right?" Emily begs.

"Sorry, hon," says Frieda. "I'm too *retro* for such things."

"Well, I'm going!"

"You can't go by yourself," Frieda warns. "They still haven't found that guy . . ."

"Ava will come with me, won't you, Ava?" Emily winks at me.

"Well . . ." I still feel frozen.

I'm beautiful?

"You have silver on your cheek—you'll fit right in!"

"I don't know . . ." I touch my hand to my face. The smear of makeup feels warm and sticky, like blood.

"There will be tons of drums and stuff, right? You're a drummer, right?"

"It would be nice to hear some music, I guess . . ."

"Cool!" Emily jumps up. "I'm going to go change!"

I hang around while Frieda and Ray close the Aloha down.

"I think I'll go pick up that video before it gets too late," Ray says to Frieda. "Be careful on your way home, all right?"

"I'll see you in a bit." Frieda gives him a smooch and locks the door behind him.

"I don't know why I said I'd go to this thing." I slide the flyer around on the counter.

"It should be fun." Frieda collapses into the stool next to mine. "Just don't let Emily get in too much trouble."

"I'll try not to."

"'The Torres-Martinez Reservation,'" she reads from the flyer as she unscrews a salt shaker cap. "Jeniece's dad was from there."

"Really?" I hand her the carton of salt. "Are you still in touch with him?"

"He's long gone, honey." Frieda pours in the crystals, twists the lid shut.

"Did Jeniece ever know him?"

"He took off right after she was born." She opens another lid. "Couldn't handle the fact that she had so many problems. I haven't heard from him since. We were never that tight anyway. Not like me and Ray."

"Does Jeniece ask about him?"

"She thinks her daddy was a migrant worker," says Frieda. "I told her we had a fling when he was here picking spinach in the valley. I told her I didn't even know I was pregnant until he had already moved on."

"And you feel okay about that?" My heart starts to pound. I know I have no right to pry, but I can't help myself.

"About what?"

"Lying to your daughter." My heart thrums even harder.

"Honey." Frieda keeps pouring the salt as she looks at me, keeps pouring it long after it spills over the lip of the shaker. "She's much better off not knowing what a no-good shit-head that dad of hers was."

"Don't you think she'd want to know where she really comes from?" I remember the burial mound Jeniece built. Maybe she has some inkling already, knowledge prickling up in her muscles, her bones . . .

"She's from the Salton Sea, and she's like the Salton Sea. That's all she needs to know." The salt keeps pouring. It forms a pile on the counter.

"In what way?"

"She was made by mistake," Frieda says.

I feel a twinge in my belly.

"I mean, it was a good mistake. Think of all the birds that come here on their way to Mexico. They wouldn't have a place to rest if it wasn't for that mistake."

"It's more of a final resting place right now, Frieda." The pile of salt is almost as high as the shaker.

Frieda follows my gaze to the counter. "Would you look at that?!" She stops pouring. "Why didn't you say anything, Ava?"

"I'm sorry . . ."

Emily bangs on the door. Frieda shakes her head as she goes to unlock it. I sweep the pile of salt into my hand and dump it in a dustbin, then brush the rest off on my pants. Emily sashays in, wearing a black mesh tank top with a lime-green bra underneath, a short patterned skirt in blues and yellows and high-heeled gold sandals. Her makeup is cranked up to a new pitch, her hair piled high on her head.

"Are you ready to get down?" She shakes her hips.

In my car, Emily jabbers away about who knows what, but all I can think about is Frieda and Jeniece. Jeniece, who thinks her father bent over rows of spinach, pulling green leaf upon green leaf out of the earth. Jeniece, whose father himself is rooted to the same patch of soil.

My mind reels. I knew mothers could be silent, I knew mothers could keep things tamped down inside themselves, but I didn't know mothers could tell such big lies. Did my mother make up the stories she sang to me, the ones I've been writing down, the ones that have been tearing me up? We never talk about those stories outside our *pansori* sessions. We act as if they don't exist, aside from in the song, in the drum, in my pen, but I can always feel them, rattling under our skins, ready to spill. What if her story, my story, has a completely different rhythm than what I had been led to believe? What if my father is not a total mystery, but someone with a name, an address, someone I could easily track down?

"Turn here," says Emily, and I crank the wheel so hard, I almost run us off the road.

The hills glow in the distance, a strange pink sheen, as I follow the tire ruts down a stretch of sandy dirt. A few cars pass us, showering my windows with pebbles. Kids whoop inside, heads rocking, arms pumping the air. They look scary to me, vaguely sinister.

"Emily, I don't know if this is such a good idea." I check the rearview mirror to see if it's safe to turn around.

"No, you're right, it's not a good idea." She sighs and reaches one leg over the hump between our seats. "It's a fucking fantastic idea!" She presses her gold heel onto the accelerator. The tires spin madly; the car lurches forward.

"Emily!" I press the brakes, sending us fishtailing over the dirt.

"Just kidding, sheesh!" She pulls her foot back, turns on the radio, and starts bopping to the ranchero music that blares out. Another rhythm—a driving techno beat—seeps into the car from the outside. I can feel it more than hear it, the rhythm pounding erratic as my heartbeat as I manage to gain control of the steering wheel again.

The dirt road curves; the pink glow intensifies. We reach a makeshift parking lot. Tents are scattered among the cars. A few kids sit on beach chairs; others lie on the ground looking at constellations. When we get out of the Sonata, the music hits me full force, electronica buzzing my breastbone. Emily grabs my elbow and pulls me toward the sound.

The wind is insane. Emily's carefully blow-dried hair flies all over the place. I can feel my own hair grow heavy with sand. A bunch of people, I notice, are wearing surgical masks. I think of my mother in her mask, protecting her lungs from eggshell dust. I clamp my lips shut tight, shield my face with one of my hands. The music is incredibly loud, and fast—at least 120 beats per minute. My heart rate speeds up in response as we walk toward it.

Even in this wind, people are dancing like crazy, jumping up and down, swinging limbs at wild angles. It seems like almost everyone is wearing huge pants—the legs so wide, they look like ball gown skirts. Lots of people are glowing, bright tubes looped around their heads, necks, wrists, neon paint all over their skin. Some people on dunes and rock formations swing glow sticks from the ends of ropes, tracing arcs, circles, blazing figure eights in the air. Several people have silver faces. Several have pink hair.

On the stage, alien cowgirls do a spastic square dance. Lights swivel from the scaffolding, sending shafts of color across the desert. Emily starts to circle her hips, slowly, not at all in time with the music—more like she's listening to some burlesque number inside her head. A few people come up to her to compliment her "totally eighties" clothes. She looks confused but flashes them a smile anyway. Everyone is smiling here—you can see it even with their surgical masks on, even with the way they squint against the wind. It hurts my face to see so much smiling. It makes me feel even worse. All I want is to go back to my trailer and go to bed.

"I'll be right back!" Emily yells over the music.

"What?" I stare at her. "You're not going anywhere! How will we find each other again? There must be a thousand people here."

"Just go over by that tarp thing." She points to the DJ booth. "I'll come right back, I promise."

"But . . ."

She waves and slips into the crowd. I head over to the tarp. The DJ has pretty impressive equipment—two DAT machines, a mixer, two turntables, two CD players. I envy the headphones clamped over his ears. He's off in some world of his own, head bobbing like one of those figures on a dashboard. He has no idea I'm standing here, wishing I could get my hands on his DATs. I finger the small tape recorder inside my purse.

Everywhere I look, people are hugging each other. I don't think I want anyone to hug me, but an all too familiar feeling of invisibility kicks me in the stomach. I don't know what I want anymore. I stick my head outside the tarp; my face is blasted with sand.

"Ava!" Emily comes running. "See? I told you I'd be right back!"

I am surprised by how glad I am to see her. Maybe we can head back home now.

"I got some X!" Emily is breathless. I can tell she's already taken the stuff—her eyes are extra wide and I can see more of her teeth than usual. She hands me a water bottle. There is so much grit in my mouth, I am happy to have a nice long drink.

"Have you ever tried Ecstasy?" she asks.

"No, and I have no intention to ever do so, thank you very much."

Emily bursts into giggles. "Too late!" She slaps her hands on her thighs.

My stomach dips.

"I just dosed you!" She can't stop laughing.

"What?!"

"I put it in the water bottle!"

"Emily!" I spit out what's left in my mouth. "What should I do? Is there an antidote or something?"

"Just enjoy it, Ava," Emily says. "You need to loosen up!" She lifts up her arms and starts jumping up and down to the DJ tracks. A group of teenage boys gather around her.

"Emily!"

She is too busy showing off for the boys to answer.

I don't know what to do. I race over to the closest tent. A bunch of kids are lounging around inside, sucking on pacifiers. I can't bring myself to ask them anything. I run over to three relatively normal-looking guys sitting on beach chairs.

"Excuse me?" I ask, panting. "Can you help me? I just took some Ecstasy!"

A hefty guy with a goatee and a kind face stands up and slips a surgical mask over my nose and mouth. The inside is slick with Vicks VapoRub. It smears on my skin, makes the inside of my nose burn. I flash on the night of the smell party, Abby's fingers, Darryl's eyes. I take a deep breath and start to cough.

"Does this counteract it?" I ask, my voice muffled.

"No, man," the guy smiles, "it *enhances* it!"

I rip the mask off my face.

"What?!"

"It makes you feel it better. I thought that's what you wanted." He adjusts his ski cap.

I run off, furiously rubbing the slick stuff from my face. I don't know where to go. The music is so loud, I can feel my diaphragm vibrate inside my ribs.

I push myself through the crowd and into some open space. The air is wild, a mad rush of prickly seeds and candy-wrapper scraps. My body begins to feel funny, like my bones are melting, like the wind can pass right through me. Only my feet feel solid, slogging through the sand. I climb up a dune. A small crowd gathers by a bonfire at the bottom on the other side, nestled in a grove of cottonwood trees. The leaves shimmer in the firelight, flashing silver like some sort of code. I can hear a single voice singing, the shake of a rattle. The techno music recedes into the background. I stumble-slide down the dune, my body streaming in all directions.

My mother balances on a star at the far edge of the Milky Way. The swirling swath shimmers between us, a river of glitter in the dark. From where I stand on my own small star her body blinks in and out of focus, but the nightingale that hovers over her head shines in sharp relief.

"I can teach you a song," I hear the bird tell her, and my mother's voice floats out into the empty space.

A crane touches down next to me and whispers, "I can teach you a dance." It lifts its strange ankles, and my hands involuntarily slap against my drum.

Crows and magpies swarm the milky span and spread their wings. Their bodies drown out all the glimmer. "Use us as a bridge," they say, then clip their beaks to each other's tails and wings, weaving together a huge hammock of bird. I place a blind foot on a crow's back. The bird bobs down, then rises back up, like a buoy. I move my other foot onto a magpie's wing. The ridges of its feathers are jagged; my foot slips, knocks against another bird's skull. I'm scared I might fall; there is nothing to hold on to but my drum as I slowly step from one bird to another. A few bright specks seep up between their wings, but it is too dark to see anything else. I can't tell whether my mother is navigating this bridge, too, trying to reach me halfway.

I wake up to a strange, buttery light—much softer than the light in the trailer, where even the sun seems harsh and fluorescent. Outside the window, a hummingbird hovers over a bird of paradise plant, then darts away, an emerald flash. Beyond it I can see hills, cactus. I'm on a futon, covered by a down comforter. The room smells of cedar and coffee. I have no idea where I am. My head pounds. My mouth is completely dry.

"Good morning." Darryl kisses my cheek. "It's so amazing to see you here."

I sit up fast. The cover slides down to my waist. I'm relieved to see that I'm still wearing my clothes.

"Are you okay?" He hands me a cup of coffee. "You were really out of it last night."

I struggle to remember what happened. Then it all comes back to me in a rush: a bunch of rave kids sitting in a scraggly semicircle on the ground, the cuffs of their enormous pants pooling together in the sand. In front of them, by the fire, a woman, around sixty years old, sang in a language I'd never heard before. She danced in small steps, half bent over, her arms and hands shaping the song. A younger woman, maybe in her twenties or thirties, obviously related to the singer, sat on the ground, shaking a large gourd rattle. She watched the singer intently as she accompanied her. My heart pounded. I fished around in my purse for my small tape recorder and pressed the red record button. I wondered if the singer was telling the truth; I wondered if the other woman hung on every word, if they rang inside her long after the song ended. I felt myself melt into the music, into the sand.

"Ava?"

I looked up. The warmth of the bonfire flooded my body.

"Darryl!" I grabbed his hand and pulled him down to the ground next to me. "I didn't expect to see you here!" My cheeks hurt, all of a sudden I was smiling so much.

"I heard there were going to be bird songs tonight." His voice was quiet so that he wouldn't disturb the singer. He looked down at our hands, linked together, and cleared his throat. His hand felt so good. I lifted it up and kissed it. *Did I really do that?*

"This is a bird song?" I whispered. I was melting, melting.

"Traditional Cahuilla," he said. "Only a handful of people still know the language . . ."

"I don't know the language of birds," I told him. "My mother told me to say I know the language of birds, but I don't!" I started to laugh.

A bunch of rave kids turned to me and said, "Shhhh!"

"Are you okay, Ava?"

"I'm fiiiine." I flopped my head against his shoulder. His shirt smelled wonderful, like soap and fire smoke. *Oh my gosh . . .*

I felt his arm stiffen. "Did you take something?"

I nodded. "Emily tricked me." I laughed even harder.

The singer spread her arms like wings. I wrapped my arms around his waist.

"Ava, this is weird," Darryl said. "You're not yourself. Maybe I should take you home."

"But I want to hear the music . . ." I pressed my ear against his chest. *Did I actually do that?*

"Ava . . ." Darryl's eyes were confused. He'd been wanting me to touch him, he's been wanting to touch me, for weeks, but now he pulled away.

I brushed the back of my hand against his hair. I wanted to say something, but I couldn't. My jaw clamped shut tight; my teeth ground together, my mouth suddenly turned dry, salty as soup mix. Only a growl could pass through. *This really happened. How could this have really happened?*

"Are you okay?" Darryl looked panicked. I shook my head. Something between a laugh and a cry bubbled up inside my chest.

"Don't sweat it." The guy sitting next to me squeezed my jaw at the hinge and opened my mouth. He slid in a pacifier, slick and wet, tasting faintly of candy. I wanted to spit it out, but it felt nice to have some space between my molars, some saliva beginning to flow.

"First time on X?" he asked me. I nodded.

"Wait till you have sex." He looked at me, then Darryl. "You'll flip out."

Even in the dark, I could see Darryl flush.

"Let's go," I whispered, the pacifier still in my mouth. Then I stood up too fast, and the world disappeared.

I pull the covers up over my chest. I'm too embarrassed to even acknowledge the night before. I have no memory of anything after the bonfire.

"I thought you lived in a tent," I say, feeling like a complete idiot.

"I'm just staying down there during the rescue effort," he says. "I want to be close by in case anyone needs me. This is my regular house. I come up here to unwind."

"It's nice," I say, and it really is, full of space and light. Through the open bedroom door I can see the main part of the house, the high open beam ceiling, the simple furniture.

"I picked it up for a song." He sits down on the bed next to me. The mattress tilts; my hips slide toward him; I try to hold them back. "It's all solar. There's so much sun out here—it makes sense to take advantage of it."

I take a sip of coffee. Is it possible he put ginger in it? It tastes amazing.

"My hat goes off to anyone who can live here," I say, but this house, this view, away from the stink of the shore, seem surprisingly, wonderfully livable.

"I really thought I wouldn't be able to hang—I'm a northern California boy, so this is a pretty intense climate for me—but they need me here. The birds. And the place has grown on me, actually. It's where I'm supposed to be right now."

I wonder what it's like to feel such certainty. My body has a hint of it—my skin feels warm, almost like it's glowing from the inside out; I wonder if the Ecstasy is still circling through my blood, or if it's just the coffee, or maybe it's from being in Darryl's bed, from Darryl being so close. It's scary, how good it feels. I'm not sure I can handle it.

"You know, there's a bird song about the first people who came to this area," Darryl tells me. "Maybe the woman sang it last night—I don't know Cahuilla, so I wouldn't have recognized it. I've just read that this song is supposed to be about the first people who came here, the first people on earth, supposedly. They could fly, so the mythology goes. They circled this place three times before they decided to touch down, to try to make a human world."

"I did that." I take another sip. "I mean, I didn't fly, but I drove around the sea three times before I decided to stay."

"I'm glad you decided to stay, Ava." Darryl leans toward me. He closes his eyes; his lips reach for mine.

I jump up, spilling the coffee all over the bed.

"I should probably go." My heart is hummingbird-fast.

"Ava . . ."

"I'm sorry about the spill—I hope it doesn't stain."

"I'm not worried about the spill," Darryl starts.

"I'll pay for it, I promise." I race toward the door.

When I get outside, I realize I have no idea where I am. My car is nowhere in sight. There is no discernible road, even, just ruts on the hill where Darryl's Jeep has gone in and out.

"Let me give you a lift." Darryl comes outside, holding my purse. He is still wearing pajamas. "I can take you home, or I can take you to your car. Just let me know what you want."

"I don't know . . ." I want to sit down on the dirt and cry.

"You don't need to go," he says. He stands a step closer. I can feel heat move between us like a hand. I close my eyes.

"Oh my gosh!" I step back. "Emily! I gave Emily a ride to the thing last night! She had no way to get home!"

"If I know Emily, she found a way," Darryl chuckles.

"You know Emily?"

"Who doesn't know Emily around here?"

"Could you take me to my car, please?" I was supposed to be keeping her out of trouble, not falling into trouble myself. "I want to make sure she's okay."

"Sure thing." He hands me my purse. "Hop in."

At the site of the rave, only a few stragglers, a few tents and cars remain. At first I can't find my car; then I see it has been turned into some sort of art piece. The top is covered with glitter. A few beer bottles and candles sit altarlike on the hood, along with a couple of condom wrappers. The top of the trunk is littered with flowers and surgical masks. The car is so spattered with dirt from the unpaved road, I can barely tell it's green. In the dust on a window, someone has written the word "beautiful." I stand, frozen, before it.

"I'll work on cleaning this up," says Darryl. "Why don't you look around for Emily."

"Are you sure you don't mind?" I ask. "I've given you a lot to clean up already."

"It's my pleasure." He smiles. "And it's true." He points to the dusty word.

It is eerily quiet here, eerily still, after the wind and noise of last night. My sternum has some sort of Pavlovian response—I can feel it buzz as if the music is still thumping through the air. I can't find Emily among the small clusters of kids sitting on the sand or in beach chairs, toasting marshmallows for breakfast and drinking sodas and beer. I peer inside the few tents that are open. Many kids sleep with pacifiers in their mouths, huddled together like puppies. In one tent, a girl with pink hair—the girl from the Aloha,

I'm pretty sure—is asleep, naked. Her pants are on the ground outside, baby-doll eyes wide open on the knees. I try not to look at her nipples, but I can't seem to help myself—she must have dyed them; they are almost as pink as her hair. Her eyes fly open; I race away, wondering where Silver Face is, wondering if I still have silver smeared on my cheek.

Darryl is lifting a condom wrapper off the hood when I get back.

"She doesn't seem to be here," I tell him, blushing. "Maybe we could check the Aloha."

"That's the restaurant you always go to, right?" he says. "I still haven't checked that place out."

"The food's not the best, but it's homey," I tell him.

"Are you sure you don't just want to go home?"

"I want to see if Frieda knows where she is," I say.

"Okay," he says. "I could use some breakfast, anyway. I'll follow you there."

I've never been so aware of the back of my head before, the backs of my arms. I can feel Darryl driving behind me, his car bouncing on the same potholes as mine, changing lanes when I do to stay right behind me. I'm glad I'm surrounded by so much metal. My body feels way too soft and fluid and warm to hold itself together.

The Aloha is surprisingly busy—at least half a dozen tables are filled, the most I've seen at one time. Emily is sitting at the counter. Relief floods through me at the sight of her. She looks at me, then quickly glances away.

Darryl touches my elbow. It feels funny to be here with him;

it's always been the place I've gone when I've wanted to avoid catching his eye. One wall crumbles down after another . . .

Frieda runs up to me and gives me a hug. Her hair smells like bacon. "Ava!" she cries. "We were so worried about you!"

"I think I passed out, but I'm okay." I glance over, but Emily won't look at me.

"*I* didn't pass out." Emily fiddles with her fork. "You only had a little bit—I barely put anything in the water."

"Did you give her something?" Frieda spins toward Emily.

"I just wanted her to relax," she says, her face pale. "Looks like it worked." She gestures to Darryl's pajamas with her head.

"Emily! How could you do something so stupid? That's totally illegal!"

"Don't lecture me, Frieda, okay?" Emily storms off to the bathroom.

"I didn't know she did that," says Frieda. "That's bad. That's really bad. That's not even what I was worried about, though—not before now, at least. We heard another body was found, not too far from that rave."

"Oh, no" tumbles out of my mouth, Darryl's mouth, together.

"When Emily said she couldn't find you last night, I got scared . . ."

"I had no idea," I tell her. "I'm glad Emily got home okay."

"Yeah, well," Frieda says, distracted. "Oh, we got some other news from the cops, too—that first body, the one you found, Ava? Turns out she was a hooker."

My heart falls to my knees.

"I didn't even know we had prostitutes in these parts." Frieda hands Darryl a laminated menu. She knows I don't need to look at the menus anymore.

"World's oldest profession," Ray says from the grill. "They're everywhere you go."

find the person who killed those people, either. I shift into reverse.

A head pops up from the bundle, and a scream involuntarily tears through my throat. I press the gas. The tires spin fruitlessly in the dirt. The person sits up; the metal pan of the lift tips back and forth. The person grabs on to the chains.

"Come on, come on," I tell the car. "Go, go, go, go!" Then I catch a glimpse of the person's face, the shape of the person's shoulders. I suddenly feel like I've been drenched in cold water. I throw the car back into park.

"Omma?" I whisper.

My mother shakily lowers herself to the ground. The tray of the lift swings. Jumbled clothes, shoes, a birdcage covered with a towel remain on it, along with a few pillowcases filled with hard-looking things.

"Your hammock work wrong."

"It's not a hammock, Omma." I walk toward her, my limbs fizzing with adrenaline. "It's like an elevator. To bring stuff up to the trailer."

"Hard on the back." She rubs her spine. She seems to be wearing several layers of clothes.

"Omma, aren't you hot?" As usual, it's at least a hundred degrees today.

"It's more easy to carry this way."

"Don't you have any bags?"

She just shrugs. I turn the key and push the button to send her scraggly pile up to the trailer. I want to ask her what she's doing here, but my tongue has retreated into silence; the effects of the Ecstasy have evaporated completely, it seems.

"Watch for Yukam!" she yells. The birdcage wobbles a bit but stays upright.

"How did you get here?" I ask. Her car is nowhere in sight.

"Anchee drive me," she says.

"Is she here, too?" It looks like someone could be hidden under the stuff on the slowly rising lift.

"She drive back home. Why you give me so many questions?"

"I'm sorry, Omma. I just wasn't expecting to see you today. You caught me off guard." *This is my mother. My mother was a prostitute. This is her. This is real.*

She reaches inside two layers of pants, pulls a tattered article out of the pocket closest to her skin, and hands it to me. My name is there, in smudged newsprint: "The body was discovered by San Diego native Ava Sing Lo, 25." I'm surprised my mother hasn't put this inside her Book of Dead Birds yet. I'm even more surprised to see myself listed as a San Diego native. I've lived there all my life, but I've somehow never considered myself native to the city, never thought anyplace could ever claim me as its own. I've always felt alien there. I've always felt alien no matter where I go.

"They think you kill her," she says.

"No, Omma, they don't," I tell her. "No one thinks I've killed anyone."

"You watch out," she says. "They think you kill her."

I scan the article quickly to make sure there aren't any accusations that I'm not aware of, but the paper gives no indication of this.

"Omma, why would anyone think I killed that woman?"

The lift shudders as it reaches the top of the chain. A stuffed pillowcase wobbles at the lip; the contents begin to spill from it like vomit. A few stray feathers take to the air. A large dark square zooms down toward me. I jump back; it lands with a thunk at my feet. Some papers fly out, some seeds and scraps of paper. It's my mother's scrapbook. I bend down and try to pick up all the loose things that have fallen out. My mother stares at me as if I've just killed another bird.

"I'll fix it, Omma, don't worry," I tell her. She looks at the feathers from Kane and Lee Lee, along with a sunflower seed hull and part of a candy wrapper, in my hand. She runs for the ladder.

"Omma, there's not much of a ledge up there," I tell her. "Let me unlock the trailer before you go up."

She creeps up to one of the highest rungs anyway and puts a protective hand over the top of Yukam's cage. She could easily fall. My heart feels like it's full of bees. I think about Darryl's house, the easy, buttery light, and wonder why I was so fast to run away.

Ava, daugher, 12,
come home from school,
give me this on yellow paper:

A siege of herons or bitterns
A wisp of snipe
A desert of lapwings
A sord of mallards
A skein of geese (flying)
A muster of peacocks
A murder of crows

[Part of yellow page torn off, taped in,
"A murder of crows" written
across it in loopy script]

11/2/83

I am not able to get much sleep with my mother in the trailer. I finally drift off in the wee hours of the morning, but am awakened shortly afterward by the smell of morning-after soup, made with sheets of seaweed and various kitchen implements my mother brought in a pillowcase. The smell makes me want to cry; I have to hide my face in my hands after I take the first taste.

"I'm teaching a self-defense class this morning, Omma." I set down my spoon. "You can stay here or you can come with me. It's like tae kwon do, for women. For women to protect themselves."

She gives me one of her sidelong glances, then snorts. "*You* teach this class?"

We haven't talked about tae kwon do since I was sixteen. I had stopped going to class after my teacher's son grabbed my breasts once after practice. I didn't tell my mother about this; she never knew why I refused to go back. After two weeks, she tricked me—she said we were going to go clothes shopping, a rare event—and drove me to the *dojang*. I refused to get out of the car. She tried to pull me out, but I was already six inches taller than my mother's five-foot frame, and thirty pounds heavier than her hundred. I didn't budge, even though I knew the teacher and his son were watching from the door of the storefront. My mother screamed at me, but I crossed my arms in front of my chest and wouldn't move.

My mother eventually exhausted herself and sat down on the sidewalk. My teacher came outside and helped her into the back of the car. She lay down across the seat and fell asleep, or pretended to, immediately. Embarrassed, I nodded my thanks, then slid over to the driver's side of the car and strapped on the seat belt. I was so eager to leave, I didn't scoot the seat back. By the time we got home, my legs were cramped from trying to fit into my mother's position. I had to shake them out and slap them to bring them back to life.

My mother brewed a pot of peacock tongue tea after we got home. We sipped from our cups together on the couch, but neither of us said a word.

I didn't practice tae kwon do again until graduate school, when I noticed classes were offered at SDSU. I was amazed by how glad I was to be doing crescent kicks and down blocks and the crane stance. My body remembered everything. I didn't tell my mother I had taken it up again. I practiced in secret in my room.

My mother slurps up the last of her soup. "I go with you," she says, a glitter of challenge in her eyes.

The self-defense group has dwindled the last couple of weeks. The bridge ladies decided, in their words, that they can now sufficiently "kick ass" and have gone back to their cards, and Rayanne never returned after Emily's comments about her boyfriend. Most weeks it's been just me, Frieda, and Emily, with Lonnie showing up every now and again.

The Aloha smells of sausage and syrup when we walk in. The breakfast crowd, if you can call three men a crowd, is still there, huddled together over their last cup of coffee. Jeniece is there, too, sitting by herself in a booth. She looks away before I can wave hello.

"Frieda, Ray, Jeniece, I'd like you to meet my mother." My mother stands behind me. They probably can't even see her.

"Howdy!" Ray lifts a spatula in greeting.

"Ava! I didn't know your mother was coming out!" Frieda wipes her palms on her apron and steps around me. "So nice to meet you," she says. My mother stands stiffly, shakes hands with Frieda like a robot.

Emily comes through the front door wearing a grayish sports bra and faded paisley bicycle shorts, holding a frayed hand towel. I almost can't look at her. Darryl put his lips on her lips. Darryl touched her skin. I feel nauseous just thinking about it.

"Emily, look! This is Ava's mom!" Frieda calls out.

"I didn't know your mom was Japanese." Emily drops her towel and stares at my mom like she's part of a sideshow. "Ava, I didn't know you were part Japanese!"

"Korea," my mother says. "I from Korea. No Japan."

"She speakee English!" Emily squeals.

"Emily!" Frieda glares.

My mother looks almost frantic. "Where you put your eggshells?"

"*My* eggshells?" Emily points to herself. "I don't have any eggshells!"

My mother turns to Frieda. "What you do with them?"

"We toss them out, I guess," she says as she gives the men their change.

"Why you not blow them?"

"You blow eggs?" Emily laughs. "Ooh, your mom's dirty, Ava!"

The three men drool at Emily before they get up to leave. She pretends to ignore them but tilts her hips in their direction. Is that what Darryl likes?

"My mom makes art out of eggshells," I say quickly. "She puts a pinprick on each side and blows the stuff out. She makes amazing stuff."

"We did that once," Jeniece pipes up. "Me and Ray. Remember, Ray? That Easter? We blew the stuff out of the eggs."

Ray winks at her.

"The house smelled like vinegar for days," says Frieda.

"Can't raw eggs make you sick or something?" Emily asks. Half her attention is on the men walking out the door. She runs her fingers through her hair to maximum effect. Is that what drew him in? "They give you botulism or something?"

"That's what the birds have," I tell her. I'm sure there's more vinegar in my voice than necessary.

"Well, the birds have eggs!"

"I think it's salmonella . . ."

"Oh! Knock knock," says Ray.

"Who's there?" Jeniece asks.

"Sam and Ella. I mean, Sam and Janet."

"Sam and Janet who?"

"Sam and Janet Evening," he sings.

"I don't get it," says Emily.

"Some enchanted evening," he sings again. "Sam and Janet Evening. Sam and Ella Eeeeevening . . ."

"You work here?" my mother asks. Ray scrapes the grill to the tune of the song.

"I eat here," I tell her.

"Where the tae kwon do?"

"Oh, the self-defense class—that's here, yes."

"You know, Ava," Frieda says. "I don't think we can do the class today. I have to take Jeniece to the doctor and we're going to have to lock everything up. I'm sorry—I should have called you."

"Damn, Frieda!" Emily picks up her towel and dabs her forehead. "I was gonna kick your butt today, too!" Did he touch her butt? Did she touch his butt? Where did they touch each other? His house? Her trailer? The fish bone–studded shore?

"Sorry, kiddos," Frieda says. "This was the only time we could get her in. We better get ready to skedaddle."

"What do you make with your eggs?" Jeniece asks my mother. My mother walks over to the booth.

"Purse, box, ship in bottle, many kinds things." She sits down across from Jeniece.

"I can't picture it," Jeniece says.

"I show you sometime," she says. "You a sick girl?"

Frieda rushes over to the booth. "Jeniece isn't sick," she says. "She just has some problems."

"I'm defective," Jeniece says.

"A birth defect doesn't mean you're *defective*," Frieda says.

"Mom, look at the word, okay? It's the exact same thing."

"I use *all* the eggshells," my mother says. "Defect one, broken one. I make things with all the one."

"Mosaics," I say, remembering the picture frames she spangles with tiny bits of shell, intricately pieced together.

"See? You're not defective," says Frieda. "You're a mosaic."

Jeniece rolls her eyes behind her thick glasses.

"I show you sometime," my mother says.

"We better go," Frieda says. "It was so nice to meet you." She shakes my mother's hand again. "Come on, Jeniece."

Jeniece tussles with her canes and pulls herself out of the booth. "See you later," she says to my mother. My mother nods and smiles. I can't remember when I last saw her smile.

"Well, Omma," I say. Her face drops when she looks at me. "Do you want to see the bird hospital?"

"If you want," she says.

"I want to do whatever you want."

She shrugs, watching Jeniece stomp-drag her way to the door. Emily watches my mother.

"So, what brings you to the beautiful Salton Sea, anyway?" she asks. Did Darryl call her beautiful, too? Did he spike her coffee with ginger? Did he look at her the way he's looked at me?

"They think Ava kill her."

"Who thinks you killed who?" Emily crinkles her eyebrows at me. Frieda stops at the door to listen.

"They think Ava kill that girl."

"Ava, have you been killing people?" Emily says with mock horror. "I thought you were just breaking hearts!" Me? *I'm* the heartbreaker?

Ray turns off the light in the kitchen.

"They put Ava in jail," my mother says.

"What?" Emily asks.

"No one's putting me in jail, Omma." I touch her elbow. It feels hard and dry, even through her windbreaker. "Let's go, okay?"

My mother lets me lead her to the door. I can feel all eyes on us as we walk back out into the light.

"It always so hot here?" She fans herself with her purse.

"Maybe we're closer to the sun than most places." Emily shields her face with her hand as she comes outside. Her nipples jut through her pilly sports bra. I feel a rush of shame about my inverted nipples. Who would ever want to touch such weird and backward things?

"We're farther, actually," I say, hating the snotty tone of my voice. "We're lower than the ocean here. We're about as low as we can go in this country."

"Oh, no." Emily sashays past us with a wink. "Believe me. We could go much, much, lower."

I forget to warn my mother about the stench at the bird hospital. I forget to warn her about what she's about to see. When we walk into the enclosure, she freezes. Then she starts to swoon. She sags against me, dead weight. I lower her onto a folding chair.

"Ava?" Darryl rushes up to us.

"This is my mother," I say, grateful to have her as a shield between us.

"Is she okay?"

"Omma, are you okay?"

She looks dazed.

"I guess passing out is a family tradition." Darryl tries to laugh, but I see the concern in his eyes. I try not to look at his hands.

"I not pass out," my mother says. Her voice seems to come from a tiny place deep inside her chest, a voice echoing from a well.

"I think she's just overwhelmed," I say. "She's never seen so many dead birds before." The pile by the incinerator is especially tall today.

"Let me get you some water," Darryl tells her. He walks off. I'm tempted to follow him, but I don't.

"Omma." I touch her shoulder. "I'm sorry. I should have prepared you better for this."

"You prepare me for this." She glares at me. "Your whole life you prepare me for this."

"Omma, you know I never meant . . ."

Darryl comes back with a water bottle, a bendy straw poking out the top. "Here." He bends down and offers it to my mother. "Have a sip."

She lowers her head and wraps her lips around the straw. I have to look away, it seems so intimate—the bottle resting on his knee, her practiced mouth. What did Emily do to Darryl with her lips?

"Omma, why don't I take you back to the trailer," I say. "I think you need to take it easy."

"Will you come back later?" Darryl asks me.

"I should probably stay with my mother," I tell him.

"Ava, about Emily . . ."

"We should go." I help my mother to her feet.

"You don't have to keep rushing off . . ."

"I'll see you later." We start to walk away.

"I just want—"

"We need to go," I tell him. "Thanks for the water."

"Nice to meet you," he calls to my mother as we hobble off to the car. I'm not sure which one of us is holding the other up.

There was no red ribbon around Sun's doorknob, so Helen walked into the room. Sun was curled up on her bed. A bruise peeked through the rouge on her cheek. She didn't acknowledge Helen's presence. Helen climbed onto the bed and wrapped her arms around her.

"I wish we were back in our cave," she said into Sun's shoulder. It hurt to talk, her jaw was aching so much.

Sun didn't say anything.

"Don't you wish it, too?" Helen closed her eyes so that she wouldn't see the blink of the neon sign outside; the light bled through her eyelids anyway. "Don't you wish we were back in our cave on Cheju-do?"

Sun pulled herself off the bed. Helen toppled over.

"Don't you know what happened in that cave?" Sun lit a cigarette.

"Our life happened in that cave." Helen sat up. "All our dreams, everything we told each other . . ."

"You're still so naive, sometimes, Hye-yang." Sun took a deep drag.

"What are you talking about?"

"Haven't you ever heard of April third?"

"Of course I've heard of April third."

"The April third massacre, the one on Cheju-do?"

Helen stared at Sun, confused.

"Thirty thousand people were killed, and you haven't heard about it?!"

"That isn't true," said Helen. Surely she would have heard something if that were true.

"People never talk about it!" yelled Sun. "Why can't people ever talk about anything?!"

"You're making this up." Helen rubbed her aching jaw.

"It was 1948. Rebels were hiding in our cave, Hye-yang! Whole families were hiding in our cave! But the army found them! The army found them and killed them, Hye-yang, right there, right there in our cave!" She took a swig of vodka from a canteen one of the GIs had left behind. "You know those bones we found? People!"

"Why are you saying this?" Helen asked.

"It's true! It's all true! Women were raped! Babies were killed! People were tortured, Hye-yang—buried alive, whipped like dogs!"

Helen covered her face with her hands but the neon still seeped through.

"My grandmother pretended to be retarded so they wouldn't rape her, but they did anyway! Two policemen put a plank on my mother's stomach like a seesaw and sat on either end, Hye-yang. She thought they were going to crush her to death. She was bleeding for days. She thought she'd never be able to have children. I was her miracle, she said, even though my real father was one of the rapists! The man I call Father was in Japan for a year before I was born, so how could it have been him?!"

"If this is true, why didn't you tell me before?" Helen cried.

"They told me not to tell! They told me not to talk about it! I didn't think I'd ever be able to say anything, but here I am! It's just words! It's easy!"

"My mother never said anything about this," said Helen.

"But she was there, Hye-yang! She was there! For all you know, your father was one of the rapists, too!"

"Sun," Helen started.

"Don't you see?!" Sun grabbed Helen's hands. "We're not supposed to say anything! What if we started talking about what they do to us here?! What if we started asking for better treatment?! They'd kill us! We can't talk anywhere!"

"Sun, you're scaring me," said Helen.

"Good! You should be scared!" screamed Sun. She jumped up and started to pull shirts out of her dresser drawer, fling them around the room. "This is scary! This is scary!"

Someone banged on the door. "Shut up in there!" he yelled.

"See? You see what I mean?" Sun said, her voice steely now, mascara running down her face.

Helen rubbed her jaw again. If words were inside her mouth right then, she couldn't feel them at all.

Another Audubon bird, gone.

The Parrot does not satisfy himself with cockle-burs, but eats or destroys almost every kind of fruit indiscriminately, and on this account is always an unwelcome visitor to the planter, the farmer, or the gardener. The stacks of grain put up in the fields are resorted to by the flocks of these birds, which frequently cover them so entirely, that they present to the eye the same effect as if a brilliantly coloured carpet had been thrown over them. They cling around the whole stack, pull out the straws, and destroy twice as much of the grain as would suffice to satisfy their hunger. They assail the pear and apple-trees, when the fruit is yet very small and far from being ripe, and this merely for the sake of the seeds. As on the stalks of corn, they alight on the apple-trees of our orchards, or the pear-trees in the gardens, in great numbers; and, as if through mere mischief, pluck off the fruits, open them up to the core, and disappointed at the sight of the seeds, which are yet soft and of a milky consistence, drop the apple or pear, and pluck another, passing from branch to branch, until the trees which were before so promising, are left completely stripped, like the ship water-logged and abandoned by its crew, floating on the yet agitated waves, after the tempest has ceased. They visit the mulberries, pecan-nuts, grapes, and even the seeds of the

dog-wood, before they are ripe, and on all commit similar depredations. The maize alone never attracts their notice.

Do not imagine, reader, that all these outrages are borne without severe retaliation on the part of the planters. So far from this, the Parakeets are destroyed in great numbers, from whilst busily engaged in plucking off the fruits or tearing the grain from the stacks, the husbandman approaches them with perfect ease, and commits great slaughter among them. All the survivors rise, shriek, fly round about for a few minutes, and again alight on the very place of most imminent danger. The gun is kept at work; eight or ten, or ever twenty, are killed at every discharge. The living birds, as if conscious of the death of their companions, sweep over their bodies, screaming as loud as ever, but still return to the stack to be shot at, until so few remain alive, that the farmer does not consider it worth his while to spend more of his ammunition. I have seen several hundreds destroyed in this manner in the course of a few hours, and have procured a basketful of these birds at a few shots, in order to make choice of good specimens for drawing the figures by which this species is represented in the plate now under your consideration.

My mother starts to come with me on my route. Every time we find a bird, she looks at me balefully, as if I have killed it myself. I have to keep reminding her that I'm not responsible, that I'm trying to help, but she just shakes her head and sighs. On the first day, I catch her trying to pluck some feathers from a pelican, and then a grebe—to put in her scrapbook, I'm sure—but I convince her that even the feathers need to be burned. I can see her scanning the ground for some evidence she can bring home and paste onto a page. I'd hate to see what she would write above it.

"Omma, have you heard any stories about pelicans?"

She strokes the top of a brown pelican's head with her gloved hands before I scoop it into the bag. "The girl-who-kills-the-pelicans story? That one I know."

"Omma." I stop for a moment. "I mean the myth about mother pelicans. People used to think that mother pelicans broke their own chests open with their beaks and served their babies pieces of their heart."

"You think I don't do this?" She smacks her palm against her chest. I remember my dream, the hummingbird feeder, the taste of diluted sugar . . .

In graduate school, some of my colleagues had babies. They were so hyperaware of how every little thing they did affected their children—they were worried about each second they spent away from their babies, each second they spent *with* their babies. They were certain they were setting their kids up for either a life of therapy and crime or a life of superstar genius fame and glory. I can't imagine my mother worried like that when I was an infant. She certainly didn't seem to when I was a child.

I wonder what my mother's heart really looks like. I imagine a wrinkled leather pouch, something mummified and dry; she could tear it into strips and serve it as jerky—chewy, saturated with salt. My mouth feels parched by the thought of it. I look at her, picking her way along the prickly shoreline, and wonder what my own heart must look like in her eyes. Sometimes I don't think I can feel it in my chest at all. Maybe that's why I keep turning to the drum, trying to find something, anything, that has a real pulse.

"I'm glad your mother is going with you, Ava," says Darryl when we return with our lumpy bag. "I've been worried about you going out there all by yourself."

"I don't go anymore," my mother says flatly.

"Why not, Omma?" I ask. I wonder if she's ready to get away from me, go back home.

"I go with not-dead birds now." She points to the kiddie pool full of sick pelicans.

"Well, we could definitely use more help here," says Darryl. "We'd be happy to have you. I'd love for Ava to come back and work in the hospital, too, get out of the sun a bit. Not that it's any less hot in here, but . . ."

"I like my route," I say quickly. I realize how stupid it sounds, saying I like my daily death march. I still have trouble looking at Darryl. Emily rises between us like some sort of lurid neon-tinted phantom.

"You know what's best for you, Ava." His voice is tired. I feel a blip of panic. I don't want him to give up on me, but I can't reach out. Not with my mother here. I don't want her to see me wanting anyone. Maybe that's ridiculous. I keep thinking about how Emily asked me if I had ever tried Ecstasy before. *No,* I told her, *and I don't have plans to ever do so, either.* I was so certain about it, so closed off to the possibility. What is it with me? Why can't I give myself the chance to have a little ecstasy—real ecstasy, not the drug—just because my mother has never been given the opportunity?

Darryl's name pops out of my mouth, barely louder than an exhale, but he's already on the other side of the hospital. My mother gives me a suspicious look, then turns to stare at a woman trying to wrestle a pillowcase over a pelican. Many of the Salton Sea residents have donated pillowcases to the hospital to use as pelican restraints—there is only one pillowcase in the trailer because Frieda has given so many away. I think I recognize the faded pattern of flowers, the rusts and yellows and greens.

The pelican puts up a good fight, but the woman finally manages to get the pillowcase over its head; in one swift pull, the pelican's head emerges from the hole cut into the top seam. The pelican tries to open its wings, but it is foiled by the funny little dress, the drab muumuu, it suddenly finds itself in. The bird snaps at the woman, knocks the syringe of electrolytes out of her hand. It's wonderful to see such a feisty bird, a bird with so much spunk. The woman grabs its beak and forces the tube down its throat. When I look over at my mother, she has tears in her eyes.

The two of us soon fall into a rhythm. I take her to the hospital in the morning, then leave for my route. My mother hasn't saved a bird yet; the pelicans keep dying in her hands. She seems to think I've jinxed her somehow, but it's a relief to know I'm not the only one without a magic touch. Every day, we go home for lunch together, then back to our respective bird trenches, then back home for dinner. I am grateful to eat her meals, her kimchi, again—she brought out jars and jars of it, along with her other favorite ingredients, wrapped in pants and jackets. I am grateful, too, to be able to avoid the Aloha. I don't want to see Emily, not yet. I cancel my classes for the time being, even though the killer is still at large. Frieda has left several messages on my machine, but I haven't had the energy to answer them. I keep expecting her to show up at the trailer, but so far she's giving me space.

I've been feeling very quiet. My mother and I don't talk much. I don't talk to anyone much anymore. I keep waiting for my mother to burst into song, to start a *pansori* session in the middle of the night, but so far it hasn't happened. I drum in the evenings, hoping to spark something in her, but she usually turns on her drill and does some carving, or takes Yukam's cage into the bathroom and lets him fly around for a while with the door closed. I want to know more of her story, even though I have enough notes to keep writing for a long time. Not that I've written a whole lot since she's been here.

It had become a ritual for me to write almost every day, even just a little bit, before I went to bed, or right when I woke up, but now I feel so self-conscious. I can hear my mother breathing, and it reminds me that I am writing about a real live person, that I am most likely taking all sorts of liberties with her past. Her true past is breathing right along with her; I will never fully know it, no matter how hard I try, no matter how closely I bend in to listen, how wet her exhale against my cheek.

I have all these scattered notes, these scattered words, these scattered feelings. They're like the tapes I've been making—snippets of bird squawk, snippets of engine hum, snippets of throat clearing and fork dropping and wind blowing through saltbushes. Who knows if they'll ever come together into something that means anything.

Before my mother showed up here, I used to be able to shut off my mind when I wrote about her. The words just poured through me. I almost couldn't control them. I never thought of myself as a "writer." I was more a historian, a scribe; it was almost like I was channeling.

Now the words have slowed themselves down. They come out one at a time, solid, separate; there is no longer any doubt they are coming out of me. It's a very different feeling. They catch in my throat and I feel like I'm going to choke. They catch in my hands and I have to play the drum harder to try to get them out, because the pen is not enough on its own. Still, as awkward as it feels, I have to keep writing. I have to chase these stories out of me, exorcise them from my body. From our bodies.

I find myself wanting to inject myself into the story sometimes, to scream out "Omma, don't go there" or "Omma, why can't you say anything?" as I write. I find myself wanting to scream the same things to myself. It's getting harder and harder to talk; at the same time, it's getting harder and harder to keep silent.

Even my dreams have changed since my mother has come here. She never enters my sleep anymore. Her presence in my trailer, on these pages, seems to be enough. I still can't seem to talk to Darryl, but he sometimes floats through my sleeping landscapes; when I wake up, he dissipates like mist—all I can hold on to is a color, sometimes a smell, a light pressure against my lips.

The bird dreams, I remember.

Last night, I dreamed I was standing in the water, naked. A pelican touched down on a wave in front of me. It poked the tip of its beak into the center of one of my breasts and gently drew out my nipple, like it would a worm from the soil; it did the same with the other one before it flew away. I woke up in the dark, my nipples tingling but inverted still, pointed inward toward my ribs, my lungs, my heart. I reached inside my T-shirt and pinched at my areolas until my nipples slipped out of their caves; I rolled them between my fingers until they were hard as pebbles, until I thought they might begin to glow. I started to feel a warmth travel through my body, slide between my legs, but when I reached down there, my mother made a sound, the couch creaked, and I pulled my hands away.

"Omma," I call to her. She's in the bathroom with Yukam.

She opens the door. The finch flies out. I do a quick scan of the windows to make sure they're closed. Yukam settles on the faucet of the kitchen sink.

"Whatever happened to that egg? That blue egg?" I ask her.

"Anchee have it."

"She's the one from the market, right?"

"I work with her when you was little girl."

"So the egg is okay?"

"I no want to bring in the car. Too much move it around," she says.

"It didn't break or anything?"

"Not everything break, Ava," she tells me.

"Did it hatch yet?" I ask her.

"Anchee have it," she says again. I decide not to press the issue. She scoops up Yukam and puts him back in his cage.

"Your omma is not here to help you!"

Helen woke up, disoriented, in her clothes, on Sun's bed. She could hear Sun yelling, in Korean, in the street. She looked out the window and saw Sun standing outside, wearing jeans, a GI's shirt, no shoes; she held a sign high up in the air. One word, in English, was written across it in large marker: UNFAR.

"Women, your omma is not here! We have to help each other! Women, women, we have to help each other!"

"Shut up!" a man's voice yelled from a room nearby.

"I will not to shut up!" Sun yelled in English before she switched back to Korean again. "We have to help each other! Do you think the clubs are going to help us? Do you think the U.S. Army, the Korean government, are going to help us? They check us for diseases, but do they care about us? Of course not! They just care about their precious soldiers—they just don't want their dicks to fall off! That's the only reason they want to keep us clean!"

A woman called out in response.

"Shut the fuck up!" a male voice yelled.

A few women ran outside to join Sun. Helen watched through the window, too scared to move, her heart bursting with fear and pride. Sun must not have taken any pills this morning, must not have lifted the flask. Her voice was crisp and fierce and awake.

Helen wished she could yell out to Sun, support her, but her own voice was hidden somewhere, salted away deep inside. She hadn't been able to sing for weeks. It was an effort to even talk; it was as if the words had to climb out of a dark, slippery well just to get to her tongue.

"What happens if someone beats us up?" Sun shouted. "Nothing! They get off scot-free!"

Women yelled and nodded in response.

"These men can hit us, punch us, rape us, kill us, and do they get in trouble?"

"No!" the women called out.

"We have to say this! We have to talk about this! If we stick together we can talk about this!"

Can we? wondered Helen. *Can I?*

"We have to show them that we're not just some little hole for their garbage!" Sun yelled. "We deserve to be treated like people! We are stars! We are superstars!"

Men shouted insults from the windows; the women in the street shouted back. The air was soon so thick with voices, it sounded to Helen like a million drums pounding. Then a gunshot rang out and the group of women scattered.

Sun came back to her room, breathless, followed by a few women from the crowd outside.

"Helen!" she beamed. "I mean *Hye-yang*! I won't call you by your American name, not anymore, ever! I promise! Did you hear me out there?"

Helen nodded, embarrassed that she hadn't come outside.

"We can do this!" Sun said to the women. Her eyes glittered. "If we work together, we can change things!"

The women began to speak about better cuts in pay, less barroom debt, accountability for the GIs who are their customers. Helen wanted to join in, but she couldn't even catch her breath. She looked outside at the jeeps patrolling the area. She didn't want to be in Sun's room when they came looking for her. As Sun scribbled furiously on a piece of paper, the other women looking over her shoulder, Helen slipped past her out the door.

The sky was a rich, clear blue, the air not too warm. All the voices earlier had obscured Helen's view out the window; she hadn't known what a lovely morning it was. She tried not to notice the jeeps honking at her as they passed, tried not to notice the men with their rifles, tried not to notice the way the dust from the ground jumped onto her ankles, leaving a thick rime, tried not to think about Sun in her room, starting something that Helen knew could never really work. She told herself to just soak in the sunshine for once, just enjoy the soft touch of it on her skin. She closed her eyes and lifted her face to the sky.

A blow to the hip jarred her out of her reverie before it really even began. A group of children ran past, chasing a small dark-skinned girl down the dirt road.

"*Ggum-doongi!*" they chanted. "*Ggum-doongi!*"

The girl ducked, teary, into the empty Shangri-La-La bar. The other children stood in the doorway, taunting her. "Yeah, run off to your Dark Man omma," one said. "She's nothing but a *ggum-doongi* fucker, just like you're gonna be!" yelled another. They picked up handfuls of dirt and tossed them into the dim room.

"Stop that!" Helen yelled at them.

The children turned toward her. "Are you a *ggum-doongi* fucker, too?" the tallest one sneered, his eyes a disconcerting shade of blue. "Do you have little Dark Man babies running around, stinking up the place?"

Helen spit on the ground right in front of his feet.

"Filthy whore!" The boy threw a handful of dirt in her face before he raced out of the DMZ, his arms raised in victory, the other children trailing close behind him. Helen blinked some of the dirt out of her eyes, spit some out of her mouth.

The girl stuck her head through the bar doorway.

"Are you okay?" Helen asked.

The girl just stared into space, her lips chapped, her hair a wild, frizzy tangle. A cold weight dropped down to the floor of Helen's stomach. Of course she wasn't okay. How was anyone going to be okay here?

Helen wondered if she should go back to Sun's room, see what they could do to make things better, but the more she thought about it, the more her feet refused to move in that direction. It's better to not even get our hopes up, she decided.

The girl slunk out of the doorway, her long Coca-Cola T-shirt badly stained, her legs and feet scabby and bare. She picked her way down the street, arms across her body as if she had a stomachache. Helen wondered if any of the GIs had gotten to her yet. She swallowed down the nausea that swept through her whole body like a wave. She wiped some more dirt from her face, brushed off the front of her short orange dress and headed over to Wild Ting to see if any GIs had stopped in yet for the morning.

Ava, daughter, 19.
Come into house with poem
book. She stand and read
in front of me. Her voice
big, not regular squeak voice.
Loud. Her hands flap around.
After she finish,
she put down book
and run out the house,
pages still spread open
on table. The book
heavy in my hands
when I pick it up.
These words covered
with pink pen:

And I had done a hellish thing,
And it would work 'em woe:
For all averred, I had killed the bird
That made the breeze to blow.
Ah wretch! said they, the bird to slay,
That made the breeze to blow!

Another bird? Another?

10/17/90

I am about to add another pelican, a brown, to my quickly bulging bag when the bird twitches. At first I think it's my own hand twitching, a sudden surge of pulse beneath my glove, but a tremor shakes through the bird and it falls from my grasp.

I drop the bag. Some of the beaks clack as they knock into each other, the ground. I kneel over the bird that had moved in my hands. It is nearly still on the ground, but I can see a slight rhythm thrum in the pelican's throat. I take off my glove and touch two fingers to the pulse. It is weak but steady. I spit on my hand and wipe at the pelican's encrusted eyes. A pale gray eye looks back at me warily.

Please, please, be okay, I try to tell the bird telepathically as I scoop it up. I leave the bag of dead birds on the shore, even though I know I'm going against standard protocol. I can come back for them later—they aren't going anywhere.

I run with the bird up the slight sandy embankment to my car. I put it on the floor mat in front of the passenger seat. I know I should bring the bird to the hospital, have Darryl take a look at it, but I feel compelled to go home instead.

"Hang in there," I tell the bird the whole way home. "Just hang in there, baby, please, hold on . . ."

Fortunately, the drive isn't too far from Mecca to Bombay. I lift the pelican out of the Sonata and carry it up the ladder into the trailer. It seems to get heavier and heavier with each step. I plunk it down in a heap on the floor of the shower. Still breathing, a good sign, but it can't seem to lift its head. I wet a washcloth in the small sink and wipe the pelican's eyes more thoroughly. The bird starts to shake.

"It's okay, now, just hold on. You're safe here," I turn on the shower and watch layers of silt and salt swirl off the feathers and spiral into the drain. I rub the feathers smooth beneath the water, cup my hand beneath the pendulous beak. *This bird is alive,* I think in amazement as the pelican starts to calm down, to shake less. *This bird will live.*

I turn off the water and slide the rippled vinyl doors shut.

"Don't go anywhere," I tell the pelican. "I'll be right back."

I drive back to Mecca Beach to get the bag of dead birds before I go to the hospital.

"Just a few on Mecca," I tell Darryl, as I drag the bag to the weighing area. "Seems to be slowing down."

"Glad to hear it." Darryl gives me a sad, lingering glance before he races off somewhere.

I feel like a criminal as I make my way over to the supply area and slide several tubed syringes full of electrolyte solution into my purse, along with some eye lubricant so the bird's eyes won't dry out before its eyelids can move again. I hurry away before anyone will notice the supplies are gone. They are going through them so fast, I'm sure a few won't be missed. My mother eyes me from the wading pool.

"Omma," I start.

She lifts her hand. A man comes over and carries away the now dead pelican she had been tending.

"Come home with me," I whisper. "I want to show you something."

"Is Yukam okay?" she asks.

"Yukam's fine, Omma. This is a good thing, a surprise."

She stands reluctantly and follows me out of the hospital. Darryl watches us leave.

"I'll bring her back later," I say, then grab her elbow and pull her to the car.

"Don't be dead, don't be dead, don't be dead," I chant inside my skull. I pull a clump of candied ginger from my purse and let the sharp flavor crystallize my thoughts as I zoom down the highway.

The bird isn't dead, although it is shivering in a skim of now cold water, oily droppings floating all around it. I move the bird so that the water will drain and run a warm shower to send the poop down the pipes and take the chill away. My mother stands in the doorway of the bathroom, not saying anything.

"You doing okay?" I crouch down beside the pelican. The warm water mists all over my already sweaty face. "I got something for you." I pull a syringe from my purse. "I am not an expert at this yet, so bear with me." I lean toward the pelican and fall onto the floor, drenching the side of my shirt.

"It's alive!" I say to my mom. She bites her lower lip.

"Okay, now, we got your favorite sports drink here." I'm sopping wet by now, the shower beating down upon me. "It'll give you that get-up-and-go—you'll be playing soccer in no time flat."

The pelican, to my amazement, opens up a wing. It unfolds over my head and bangs into the opposite edge of the shower stall, although it is not nearly open all the way. I feel like I'm beneath the bar awning at the Aloha Room. I scoot out from beneath the feathers.

"Come on, now," I coax. I get the tube into the bird's beak and squirt the 100 ml of electrolyte down its throat. "There you go. Much better."

"I'm just going to get some dry clothes on, okay?" I tell the bird. "You hold tight now. Make yourself at home . . ." *Oh my god, what am I doing?*

"Omma, can you keep an eye on him while I change?" I ask. She nods as I race to the bedroom. My heart is pounding so hard, I can barely use my fingers. I have to rebutton my dry shirt three times before I get the holes in the right order; I almost fall over trying to put on my pants. When I glance in the mirror, I hardly recognize myself—a shimmer seems to come off my skin, like part of me is moving so fast, so frantically, it creates a halo effect.

"It want to get out," my mother says when I get back into the bathroom. The pelican, still on its side, is flopping its one wing around. It looks much healthier than it did even a few minutes ago.

"Are you ready for some more?" I pull out another syringe. I can't remember what the timing is supposed to be with the electrolytes. It couldn't hurt to rehydrate the bird, could it?

I try to get closer to the bird, but it is beating its wing too hard. The wing seems so separate from its listless body, like a flag whipping around on top of a mountain.

I finally get underneath the wing and ease the tube down the bird's throat. It looks at me with great distrust; its wing slows down and eventually folds back into its side. For a moment I worry the bird has died, but I can see its breath rise and fall. My breath rises and falls right along with it.

The next few days are a blur of rehydration and eye lubrication, a blur of wet feathers and cautious hope. I feign illness so that I can stay home with the pelican; my mother pockets more supplies as needed during her shift at the hospital. The bird gets a little stronger every day. It can start to move its eyelids; then it can start to move its neck; then it can stand on its hocks; then it can stand on its feet. Then it begins to get feisty.

"Omma, could you get the pillowcase off the pillow on the sofa?" I ask her. "I think we're going to need it."

She nods and races out. She comes back with a pillowcase from home, the one that was filled with pots and pans when she first got here, covered with bleached-out geometrical patterns.

"We're going to need to cut a hole in it—do you mind?"

She shakes her head, then puts the pillowcase to her mouth and tries to pull the seam out with her teeth.

"Maybe we should get some scissors," I say, but she shakes her head again and yanks harder. I hear a ripping sound. She holds up the pillow. Blue threads dangle from her lips. The pillowcase gapes open—a perfectly sized hole.

"What we do now?" she asks.

"We put it over the bird's head," I tell her.

"After that. What we do with the bird?"

"I don't know, Omma," I tell her. "We'll figure something out."

"I do the bird, you do the pillow." She leans into the shower, drenching herself, sending water spraying out of the stall. The bird hits her in the face with its beak. She pulls her head back out; a bit of blood trickles next to her eye.

"Are you okay, Omma?" I ask.

"I fine." She leans in again. I lean above her and turn off the shower. I try to put the pillowcase over the bird's head, but it is moving around too much. A wing smacks my mother in the mouth, cutting her lip.

"This bird very not-dead," my mother says.

"Yeah—hopefully we can manage to stay not-dead in the process ourselves," I tell her. I get the pillowcase partially on the bird, but I can't get it all the way over. An eye peers out of the head hole like a child dressing up like a ghost for Halloween. I rustle with the cloth until the gap slides over his wet skull; the pillowcase bunches up like a collar around his neck, his wings still free beneath it.

"Omma, can you fold in his wings?"

"How I do that?"

"I don't know—just try!"

We struggle with the bird until finally my mother squeezes the two wings in like someone playing a concertina and I yank the cloth the rest of the way down. The pillowcase doesn't look like a dress on this bird, it looks like a sausage casing. The poor bird struggles to keep its balance, its wings tightly pinned.

"I'll try to give it some more stuff." I hold out the tubed syringe. The bird snaps and snaps, but I manage to slip the tube into its beak and press the plunger down. I'm soaking wet; my mother is sopping and bloody. We collapse back against the sink.

"I think it's ready for fish," I tell my mother.

"I think I ready for bed," she tells me.

I wet a washcloth and gently rub her temple. I smear some of the same antibiotic ointment we've been putting on the bird's "bedsores" on the cut. She closes her eyes. I don't think I've ever touched her like this before, so tenderly. I don't know if anyone ever has. I dab some more with the washcloth, wanting to keep the connection, wanting to keep touching her like this. I dab and daub until she begins to squirm.

"That enough," she says, and leaves the bathroom.

"What do you think of that?" I ask the pelican. It struggles inside its pillowcase. I ease the material back over its head and let it spread its wings.

A couple of days later, the pelican is hopping all over the bathroom, preening, roosting on the edge of the sink, knocking our toothbrushes all over the place. It is swallowing fish without spitting them back up. Its hocks are free of sores. Its eyes are clear. It is time to set it free.

My mother and I begin to make plans. We decide to drive down to Casa Cove, her old skin-diving haunt, and release it there.

"We bring the mosaic girl," my mother says.

"The mosaic girl?"

"The girl with the sticks," she says. "The girl at the tae kwon do place."

"Jeniece?"

"I think that the one."

"Why do you want to bring Jeniece?"

"She want to see my eggs."

I've barely spoken to Jeniece, other than our encounter at the burial ground. My mother hasn't seen her since her first morning at the sea. I don't know whether Frieda would want us to take her so far away, especially when we haven't spoken for a while ourselves. Still, I remember the way my mother smiled at Jeniece, the way Jeniece seemed so easy with her. "I'll talk to Frieda about it," I tell her.

"You do it soon." She points to the pelican, flapping madly on top of the toilet.

"Will you be okay alone here for a few minutes?" I ask her.

"I not alone. Go!" She shoos me off with her hands.

It feels weird to pull into the parking lot of the Aloha. It's like it's been lifetimes since I've been there, even though it's been less than two weeks. The light seems starker on the salty pavement; the bamboo sign looks shabbier than I remember. Now that Darryl has been here, I feel his not-being-here acutely. It takes me a while to touch the handle of the door, pull it open.

"Ava!" Frieda rushes up to me after I finally come in. "How are you? How's your mom?"

"We're doing okay." I want to sink into her hug, but I shrink away from it instead.

"We've been worried about you." Frieda pulls back and searches my face.

"I'm fine," I say. "I've just had some stuff to sort out." I look around the room. Much to my relief, Emily isn't there.

"I'm so sorry Emily did what she did," Frieda said. "I want you to know I've given her a good talking to."

"It's okay . . ."

"No, it's not! Giving someone drugs without telling them—there's no excuse for that! I almost called the police on her!"

I've been so focused on Emily and Darryl together that I had almost forgotten about Emily dosing me. I remembered my refusal when she first asked me about whether I'd ever tried Ecstasy more than my panic after I realized what she had done. I've tried not to let myself remember how good it felt after things kicked in . . .

"Listen, Frieda, how's Jeniece doing?"

"Jeniece? She's fine . . ." She looks at me quizzically; we haven't really talked about Jeniece before.

"Is her health okay?"

"Her eyesight is deteriorating a little, the doctor says, but for the most part, she's doing pretty good."

"Great." I'm not sure how to broach the subject. Frieda absently runs her hands over the laminated menus in their wooden pocket, fanning them out; they make a *fwap fwap* sound when they fall back in place. I almost want to ask her to do it again so that I can record it.

"Anyway," I start. "My mom and I are going to San Diego tomorrow morning—just for the day—and we were wondering if we could take Jeniece with us."

"San Diego?" Now Frieda looks even more confused.

"Just for the day. My mom wants to show her her egg carvings. Jeniece sounded pretty interested, and . . ." I can't bring myself to mention the pelican.

"I'm not sure," says Frieda. "I'd need to talk to Ray about it. And Jeniece, of course, to see if she'd even want to go."

"Sure," I say. "I know this is kind of weird, Frieda. We'd take good care of her, I promise."

"I don't doubt that, Ava. It's just that she's never been that far away from home. Other than a couple of hospitals, but one of us was always with her."

"She's never been to San Diego?"

"It's not like she hasn't ever been away from the Salton Sea or anything," she says quickly. "We've taken her to the Date Festival in Indio and stuff like that. It's just kind of hard to get out . . ."

"My mom never took me out much, either . . ."

"Anyway, I'll talk to them and let you know. I'm not promising anything but I'm not saying no."

"Thanks, Frieda. I better go . . ." I start to back away.

"Aren't you going to stay for breakfast?"

"I can't today," I tell her. "My mom is already cooking something. I'll be back soon, though, I promise. I know it's part of our deal, me eating here."

"Don't worry about that, Ava. I just like to see you around."

I feel myself start to tear up. "Well, we want to get a pretty early start tomorrow." I try to wipe my eyes discreetly. "If you could call me before it gets too late tonight, I'd appreciate it."

"I'll do that," she says. "You take care of yourself, Ava."

I nod and rush outside before I start bawling.

We plan our departure. My mother packs her things in case she decides to stay in San Diego. We hydrate the pelican. We get Yukam's cage ready. We stay up fairly late, but Frieda never calls. I can't tell whether I am sad or relieved.

In the morning, just as I start to load up the car, Frieda pulls up and rolls down the window.

"She wants to go," she says. Jeniece cowers in the backseat.

"I never said I *wanted* to go." She crosses her hands over her chest.

"Come on. It will be good for you," Frieda tells her. "A change of scenery and everything."

Jeniece scowls as she undoes her seat belt. "You just want to go to the movies with Ray or something."

"Well, we don't have a lot of time just the two of us . . ."

"So you're just going to pawn me off?"

"Jeniece, this is a great opportunity for you. You'll get to see more of the world!"

Jeniece rolls her eyes and sighs. I think I've seen her eyes rolling more often than I've seen them any other way.

"We'll have a great time!" I say, my voice a little too bright-sounding. "You'll get to see the ocean . . ."

"We have the sea right here." She opens her car door, sticks the canes out first.

"And my mom wants to show you her eggs."

Above us, my mother opens the door of the trailer. I can see the pelican scuffling around behind her. I make a motion for her to close the door. Frieda looks up after the door is shut.

Jeniece sighs again as she heaves herself out of the car, the cuffs of the canes around her forearms.

"We'll have an adventure!" I imagine this sounds like something a person should say to a child, but I don't really know. I've never really spent time with kids before. Even when I was a girl, I rarely spent time with other kids aside from school and tae kwon do class, and even then I pretty much kept to myself.

"I didn't ask to go, you know," she says.

"This wasn't an easy decision for me, either, honey," Frieda tells her. "But Ava here was so generous, and—"

"Forget it," says Jeniece. "It's fine. I'm glad I don't have to look at you today, anyway."

Frieda turns to me. "Is this a way a daughter talks to her mother?"

I'm not the right person to ask, that's for sure.

"It's fine, Mom." Jeniece's voice softens a bit. "I'll be fine."

"If she gives you a hard time, you give one right back to her," Frieda tells me.

"We'll be great," I say, even though I have no idea what I'm getting myself into.

"I love you, sweetie." Frieda kisses the top of Jeniece's head. "You be good now."

She opens her car door. "Thanks again, Ava," she yells out the window before she pulls away, spraying salt and gravel in her wake.

"She couldn't wait to get rid of me," says Jeniece.

"I'm sure that's not true," I say, but what do I know?

The door to the trailer opens. "I come out now?" my mother asks.

"I'll be right up," I tell her.

Jeniece waves at my mother; she smiles and waves back. Then the pelican tries to get outside and my mother quickly closes the door.

"What *was* that?" Jeniece asks.

"It's a pelican," I say.

"I thought so!" she says. "Why do you have a pelican in your house?"

"We've been taking care of it. It was pretty sick, but now we're going to release it."

"Today?"

"That's the plan."

"With me?"

"I didn't tell your mom because what we're doing is kind of illegal."

"Cool!"

"So why don't you wait in the shade under the trailer?" I say. "I'll go get the pelican and we'll hit the road."

"Awesome!" She shuffles off beneath the landing.

The pelican is in a pillowcase, but it's still hard to get it out the door. It will be too much of a handful to try to carry down the ladder, so I put it on the metal lift. It maniacally scrabbles around the metal square.

"It scared!" my mother yells. She steps onto the lift, sits down, and tries to hold it in her arms. The pelican gets more frantic. The lift sways dramatically. I push the button, and the metal pan falls, way too fast, to the ground. It lands with a crash just inches away from Jeniece.

"Cool!" Jeniece yells again.

"Are you okay?" I call down to my mother.

"I fine!" She grabs hold of the sack of bird before it runs away.

We wrestle the bird into the backseat floor well of the car. My mother wants to sit back there with it, but Jeniece says she can't sit in the front seat if there's an air bag. Before we even make it to the highway, the pelican starts attacking Jeniece's canes with its beak, making a great clanking sound that I surreptitiously record before Jeniece completely freaks out. I pull over to the side of the road; we move the bird to the floor of the passenger seat in front, and my mother moves to the backseat. The bird thrashes its head around occasionally, nicking my legs with the tip of its beak, getting in the way of the stick shift every now and then, but the drive is otherwise fairly uneventful. My mother and Jeniece talk intently in the backseat, their heads bent toward each other; I try to hear what they're saying, but I only catch little snippets—"egg," "mother," "bird." A song rises up in me like hysteria. I can't help but sing it out loud:

"Sing Lo, sweet chariot, comin' for to carry *you* home." I point to the pelican. Before I know it, my mother and Jeniece are joining in, singing to the bird, filling the car with music. The pelican looks confused—it slams its head against the door a couple of times, but then it settles in. I almost think I can hear it hum along.

It feels funny to pull into the Casa Cove parking lot as a driver; I've only been a passenger here before. A passenger leaving with a squirming bag full of lobsters, not a driver arriving with a squirming bag of pelican.

"Omma, do you still come here to skin-dive?" I ask her.

"I go sometime," she says. "Not so easy anymore. Not so easy hold my breath under water."

"Do you like to swim?" I ask Jeniece.

"I don't know how," she says. She looks at the ocean, awestruck. I had forgotten that she's never seen it before. I open the door and the ocean air floods the car. It smells amazing—the scent is big, open somehow, not claustrophobic like the smell at the sea, with its death stench and algae tides.

"Will you be okay going down the hill?" I ask. I had forgotten that the parking lot overlooked the beach, that there is quite a big trek both ways.

"I think so . . ."

My mother gets out and opens the door for the pelican. I open the door for Jeniece. The pelican starts to bound down the sandy hill, but with its wings straitjacketed, it keeps losing its balance and tumbling for yards at a time. My mother runs after it. I keep an eye on them as I help Jeniece sidestep down the hill, her canes slipping every once in a while, unable to find purchase. Eventually we all make it down to the bottom. I'm grateful the beach isn't too crowded—I'm sure the four of us make quite a sight. People begin to gather round.

"Why you got that pelican all trussed up?" a teenage boy asks. "Are you gonna cook it or something?"

"You should set the poor creature free!" a woman says, distraught.

"We are," I try to assure her. "We're from the Salton Sea. We just rehabilitated this pelican and now we're going to release it." I know we don't look very official, but that seems to appease her.

My mother bends down by the pelican. She gets the pillowcase partway up its body, but it thrashes around and shakes the cloth back down. I give it a try, but the pelican won't even let me get close. Finally, Jeniece lowers herself to the ground and lays her canes a few feet away. The pelican is distracted by them; my mother eases the pillowcase over its head as it tries to eat one of the metal cuffs. The pelican stretches its neck, spreads its wings. We all scooch back. It opens the feathers at the end of each wing tip like fingers. My heart starts to pound in my ears. I look over at my mother; her hand is at her throat.

The pelican starts to run. The small crowd cheers it on. The pelican runs and runs, wings open, until it gets to the water. Then it stops. It waits a little bit, then takes a tentative hop into the waves. It stays there, bobbing like a buoy near the shore, for the longest time. I want to urge it to keep going, to fly away, but it doesn't seem to know what to do. The teenage boy runs out into the water and chases it further out into the surf. It keeps bobbing there, bobbing, bobbing, bobbing. We sit on the sand and watch it for a good portion of the afternoon. I almost want to swim out there and bring it back with us, take it back to the Salton Sea, but I know how crazy that would be. We finally shout our good-byes. Only as we're making our way back up the hill, Jeniece panting with the exertion of it, does the pelican lift off and head for the setting sun.

*   *   *

The car is incredibly quiet as we drive back to the apartment. It's as if a great weight has been lifted; I thought I would feel relieved, and I do, but I'm surprised by how empty I feel, too. I'm sure my mother feels the same way. The exhilaration has yawned open into something else, something big and wordless and more than a little sad. Jeniece fidgets around uncomfortably in the backseat. I'm sure she's eager to see my mother's eggs, to get our attention focused back into something small, something with definite edges.

As we pull up to the complex, I can see the door to the apartment is wide open. My heart drops.

"Omma, did you give someone the key?"

She shakes her head.

"Did you lock the door when you left?"

"Of course I lock it!"

"Uh-oh." Jeniece's face in the rearview mirror is filled with fascination and dread.

"You don't think you left it open by accident?" I know it's ridiculous to say this—she's been gone for three weeks; even if she had left it open, a neighbor surely would have closed it by now.

"Ava! You think I not know what I do?"

"You two stay in the car." I open my door. "I'll go check it out."

Jeniece lifts up her hands in surrender. "You're the black belt," she says.

"Black brown belt," my mother corrects her. "She not make it all the way." Already it's as if the whole stirring drama with the pelican never existed.

It feels weird to go up the pebbly steps again, to see the dingy stucco walls, as if I'm stepping back into a skin I thought I had shed. I can feel my body gearing up for the possibility of a fight, my muscles gathering potential energy. I've never had to use my tae kwon do in a real-life situation before. I'm not sure I'll be able to go through with it.

"Hello?" I say as I near the open door. No response.

"Hello?" I say again. The scent of my mother's seaweed soup pours out of the apartment like an exhale, even though she hasn't been there for weeks. I peer inside, my heart perched in my throat like an Adam's apple.

The floor cushions by the coffee table are slashed and—my heart sinks at the sight of this—eggshells are everywhere, but otherwise the living room looks okay. I step through the doorway. Everything seems to be in its place. Nothing is missing, as far as I can tell. My mother's room is stripped bare, but I'm pretty sure it's because she brought everything with her when she came to see me. In my room, my mixing boards are still under my bed; my MIDI keyboard is silent on its stand. I'll have to remember to bring them back to the trailer with me. If I go back to stay any longer, that is. I'm not sure where I belong now. Probably not here. My room feels weird, fake, like the set of a TV show I once watched but am now embarrassed by. I don't feel any trace of real life inside these walls; I don't think it's only because I've been gone for so long.

I go back into the living room. Who would tear up some cushions and break some eggshells and leave? Was it kids? Cats? My mind starts to spin—maybe it's the Salton Sea killer, maybe he found out my mother was a prostitute . . .

A strange sound shakes the apartment, a weird metallic thumping.

"Hello?" I ask. No answer. I stand behind the door—which I stupidly left open—and assume the ready stance. The thumping gets louder, closer. My muscles feel ready to spring. So ready to spring, in fact, that when the sound gets even closer, like someone is clomping across the balcony with coffee-can stilts, I jump out from behind the door and let out a "Hi-*ya!*" kind of sound.

Jeniece and I scream at the same time; she scoots back and almost topples over the railing. My mother grabs her by the elbow and helps her steady herself.

"I thought you were going to stay in the car!" I can barely breathe.

"She need to pee," my mother says.

"Too late," Jeniece says. A wet patch spreads along the inseam of her pants.

"Oh, Jeniece." I usher her into the apartment.

Jeniece nods; she's trying not to cry. My mother pushes past us; when she sees the eggshells all over her room, she drops to her knees. She scoops up fragments and lets them fall again to the floor, somber confetti.

"Who do this?" she whispers.

"It wasn't me, Omma . . ."

"I know it not you! You think I think you come up here and break my eggs?!"

"I wouldn't be surprised . . ."

"I wouldn't be surprise, too, but you not do this."

"The eggs were pretty, I can tell," Jeniece's voice trembles. She bends down and picks up a piece, tendriled with carvings. The sharp scent of pee wafts up; the stain on her white pants is orange, from vitamins, maybe, or dehydration. I'll try to remember to offer her some water later.

"They pretty—they beautiful!" My mother runs her hands across the carpet; little pieces of eggshell jump up like popcorn. "They take hour and hour of work—hour and hour! All gone!"

"But you can still use them, right?" Jeniece says. "You can still use the broken ones, you said."

"This too many broken." My mother crunches some in her fist. Jeniece's face drops.

I go to look for some clothes for Jeniece to change into. Most everything would be way too big. I finally find an SDSU T-shirt that's just about the right size for her to wear as a dress.

"I hope this will be okay." I hold it out for her to peruse. "I'm afraid I don't have any underwear that would fit you, but this should go down past your knees, so I don't think you have to worry."

"Thanks." She takes it from my hands.

"Do you want to take a bath or a shower?"

"I take baths."

"Well, the bathroom is down the hall," I tell her. "Feel free . . ."

She looks hesitantly down the hallway.

"I'll get you a towel." I hope there is a clean one somewhere in the apartment.

"I don't know . . . ," she starts. "I mean, sometimes I have a hard time . . . I mean, could you maybe set up the bath for me?"

"Not a problem." Her face just about breaks my heart. "I'm happy to do it."

"I don't do this all the time, you know," she says. "I mean, we were in the car for a long time . . ."

From the floor, my mother says mournfully, "It okay. When I laugh, I wet my pants, too."

She must not wet her pants very often.

"It's certainly nothing to be ashamed of," I say. "We all do it every once in a while. I don't think we have time to run a load of laundry, but we can rinse out your pants and bring them home in a plastic bag . . ."

She nods, a little teary. I go to prepare her bath.

The bathtub is filthy, coated with dirty soap scum and hair. I find some scouring powder and the desiccated remains of a sponge under the sink and set to work. The ghosts of Estonian swans float above my scrubbing hands. I never imagined this tub would hold a girl from the Salton Sea, never imagined my Salton Sea shower would hold a pelican, never imagined I'd go to the Salton Sea in the first place.

As I fill up the tub, I can hear my mother's voice over the rush of the water. Her *pansori* voice, not her regular voice. I race out into the living room. Jeniece looks terrified. My mother's voice can get pretty scary-sounding, low and guttural and torn.

"Your bath is ready," I tell her.

"Is your mom okay?"

"This is just something she does sometimes," I tell her. "It's a Korean way of singing. She used to be a performer, a long time ago."

"Can you call my mom?" Jeniece starts to cry.

"Why don't you go take your bath and we'll call her after you get out," I say, trying to listen to my mother's words at the same time. "There's a towel hanging on the rack."

Jeniece nods tearily and sets off for the bathroom.

My hands itch for my drum. I lower myself onto a torn cushion and smack the coffee table twice.

"They kill her!" my mother wails, her voice rising and falling in wild swoops. "They kill her!"

I catch my breath and pound the coffee table again. I wonder if she's talking about the woman at the Salton Sea. I kind of doubt it.

"They break her like eggshell," she sings. "They break her. She try to help us. She make a union, and they break her!"

Pound pound slap.

"She call union Silky Domestic Fowl. Korea protect this bird, make this bird a treasure, but who gonna protect us? Who gonna make us a treasure?"

Slap pound slap.

"I don't help her. I get too scared. I don't help her. I don't help her!"

Tap tap tap tap tap tap tap.

"They say she get killed 'cause she go out with white man. She don't go out with white man! She try to get us more better life!"

Slap slap slap.

Her voice drops to a whisper. "I don't help her."

Tap.

"Sun . . ." She starts to cry.

My palms throb, but they can't respond. My mother grabs eggshells in both hands and rubs them over her face, her mouth trembling, her breath jagged. I inch over and put my arms around her. She tenses, then collapses against me, sobbing.

"Omma," I whisper into her hair. "I'm so sorry. I'm so sorry . . ."

"I so sorry," she says, but I don't think she's talking to me.

My mother decides to stay in the apartment to clean up the eggs. I unpack her stuff from the trunk and bring it upstairs before we take off for the sea. The mats in the car are completely plastered with pelican poop.

"Thanks for coming with us today," I tell her.

"It was fun," she says unconvincingly. Her hair is still wet. I can't tell if the streams running down her face are tears or bathwater.

"Are you hungry?" I ask her.

She nods her head.

We get some drive-through on the way to the highway. She's asleep before she eats even half of her burger.

It feels funny to drive back to the sea in the dark. It's almost as if I know where I'm going.

Frieda is outside, waiting for us, when we pull up to the Aloha. "Thank god you're okay," Frieda says when I roll down the window. "I was worried sick." She looks frantic. I don't know why—we told her what time we were going to leave San Diego, and we made good time. Jeniece wakes up at the sound of her mother's voice.

"Frieda, are *you* okay?" I ask.

"I need to talk to you."

"What's up?"

"Not in front of Jeniece."

"Mom . . ."

"It's grown-up stuff."

I get out of the car. Jeniece does, too, her movements slow, groggy.

"What's that you're wearing?" Frieda asks her.

"It's Ava's shirt."

"Everything's fine." I hand her the plastic bag with Jeniece's rinsed-out clothes. "Jeniece had a little accident, but everything worked out okay."

"Jeniece?! What's gotten into you?! Are you two years old or something?"

"I'm not a baby!" Jeniece screams, instantly more awake. "It was an accident! Why do you always want to pick on me?!"

"Go to your room, young lady!" Frieda yells at her.

Jeniece opens her mouth in protest.

"Now!"

Jeniece groans and clomps off.

"I was looking forward to seeing her, too," sighs Frieda.

"She's a great kid," I say. "She didn't give us any problems at all."

"I guess she just saves it for me." Frieda rolls her eyes.

I want to defend Jeniece, but I don't know what to say. "You had something you wanted to tell me? Grown-up stuff?"

Frieda's face drops. "It's Emily."

I feel queasy. She and Darryl must have run off together. Maybe they got married. Maybe she's having his baby . . .

"She's in ICU. It's pretty bad."

Despite myself, I feel flooded with relief. "What happened?"

"Someone tried to kill her. The police think it was the same guy who killed those two girls. She had the same marks on her neck."

"Oh my gosh."

"They have her boyfriend in custody, but I don't think he did it. I mean, he roughed her up a couple of times, but he's too much of a chickenshit to try and kill someone . . ."

"Why is he in custody, then?"

"He has a record. When he beat her up, I called the police on him. No way was I gonna let him get away with that. Plus, his fingerprints were all over her, and some of his semen was in her and on her lips and everything . . ."

I feel another wave of nausea.

"Are there any other suspects?"

"Not that I know of. I think the guy's out there still, I really do. I think he's close by. Maybe you should stay with us tonight, Ava."

"No, thanks," I tell her. I'm looking forward to having some time in the trailer alone. "Thanks for letting me borrow Jeniece for the day. She really is a great kid, you know."

"I know," Frieda says softly.

"I don't think she knows you know." I bite my lip.

Frieda clears her throat. "Well, anyway, thanks for taking her."

"Good night, Frieda."

"You be careful now, all by your lonesome."

"I'll be fine, Frieda. Don't worry about me. I'm a self-defense teacher, remember?"

"I don't think the class helped Emily none," Frieda says. "No offense . . ."

"None taken. Good night, Frieda," I say again, then go to the car.

When I get to the trailer, the hairs on my arms stand up. Everything looks okay—the door is closed, the lift is empty—but I feel nervous. The stress of the whole day must be getting to me. I take a deep breath and get out of the car. A rustling comes from under the trailer, where all the pipes are. I tell myself it's only a cat, only a dog, only a bird, but a person—a large person, a man—steps out of the shadows. My limbs turn fizzy with adrenaline; I shakily assume the ready stance. I wish I could see better—without the headlights, it's hard to distinguish anything, but I can tell he's coming closer, with an intensity that almost takes my breath away. When he gets within a yard of me, I jump into the air and kick him in the throat. He falls to the ground with a huge thud. I race up the ladder of the trailer to call the police and hide behind the door. A police car and an ambulance pull up. I wait until I hear a knock before I stand up. When I open the door, I recognize one of the policemen who questioned me at the station.

"So you find the bodies *and* the guy who killed them, huh?"

"I just found one . . ."

"What kind of racket do you have going on here?"

"There's no racket." I have no idea what he's talking about. He fingers his handcuff.

"You two working in cahoots? He takes the tumble for you? What's the deal?"

"I'm sorry—I don't understand . . ."

"Sure you don't," he nods slyly. "The guy down there says he knows you."

"He what?" I run to the window.

"He says he works with you."

In the squad car's headlights, I can see the man sitting up now, the back of his wavy hair . . .

"Oh, no."

"Are you two like Bonnie and Clyde or something? Or like those two in that movie with the bartender from *Cheers?* The dumb one? That movie where the couple goes around killing people?"

"Officer." Words start to tumble from my mouth. "There's been a mistake. That's my friend out there. I didn't recognize him in the dark . . ."

"Slow down," he says. I try to take a deep breath.

"That's a friend of mine," I say. "He didn't do anything. I just got scared and kicked him. I thought it was the killer, but it was just my friend . . ."

"Why don't we come down and have a little chat, then, all of us?"

I nod.

We step out onto the narrow landing together.

"Strange place you have here," he says. He goes down before me—probably to keep me from bolting.

"Darryl," I call out. "Darryl, I'm so sorry!" This seems to be my catch phrase these days—maybe it always has been: *I'm sorry.*

Darryl looks up at me and tries to smile. He is obviously in a lot of pain.

"Ava," he croaks out.

I jump off the ladder and run to him.

"I'm so sorry, I thought you were the guy . . ." I crouch down before him. He reaches out a hand. I grab it. I feel a jolt go all the way up my arm.

"I know," he says, his voice whisper-soft, strained. "I should have let you know it was me." He stops to cough; my hand falls when he lifts his to cover his mouth.

"Do you want to press any charges?" the cop asks Darryl.

He shakes his head. "It was an honest mistake."

"Is there anything I can do?" I ask him.

"Let me take you to dinner tomorrow," he wheezes, like the air coming out of a bellows. He coughs again. Some blood flies out.

"Oh my gosh, Darryl, I really hurt you."

He puts his hand to his chest and winces out a smile.

"We need to take you in," one of the paramedics says. They wheel a gurney toward him.

"And we need to ask you some more questions," the officer tells me.

"But—"

"No buts about it," he says.

"But I know the language of birds," I say. He stares at me like I'm crazy. I feel a crazy laugh bubble in my chest, but I don't let it out.

As he leads me to the squad car, I turn to Darryl, who is being strapped in to the gurney. "I should take *you* out to dinner, not the other way around . . . ," I start.

He smiles—a real one breaking through the wince—then coughs up more blood.

I drive to the hospital after the police are done questioning me, but Darryl has already been released. I want to check up on him, but I don't know his number and I don't know how to get to his house. There is a message on my machine when I get back home. "I'll be there at seven tomorrow," he says, his voice strained but amused. "In full body armor, of course." His laugh turns into a coughing fit, and then the tape is quiet. I think the message is over, but after a couple of beats he says, "I'm really looking forward to this, Ava." I can hear him breathe for a while before the tape clicks off.

I take another step on the bridge of birds. White pelicans, gray mourning doves, are scattered among the crows and magpies. I can see a few feet in front of me thanks to their light feathers, but my mother is still out of my range of vision. I hear the nightingale over her head tell her to sing; all that comes out of her mouth is breath. I wobble toward her exhale, my fingers thrumming soft.

The bridge sways under my feet. The nightingale's eyes flash in the dark. "Chosim haseyo," *it tells me from a distance.*

The birds who make up the bridge open their beaks and fly away. The Milky Way sparkles back into view, a flurry of flashbulbs. I have to close my eyes against the sudden dazzle. My mother's silhouette burns inside my eyelids. I can't figure out what's under my feet, now that the bridge is gone. I can't figure out why I haven't started to fall.

The next day goes by like a blur. I spend an embarrassing amount of it in front of the mirror. My hair has grown a lot since I've been out here. I've always kept it cut close to my skull, barely there; even when I was a little girl, my mother cut it that short. She didn't know how to deal with my hair. Mothers of black kids would shake their heads in dismay at my almost bald head. Now my hair is poufing up like a mushroom. I tie a scarf around it to hold it down a little. After changing a zillion times, I finally decided on simple—white shirt, tan pants, which I hang in the shower to steam the wrinkles out. I am trying to decide whether or not to put on earrings when I hear the car pull up. I keep my earlobes bare, take a deep breath, and go outside.

"Should I be scared?" Darryl calls up to me as I climb down the ladder.

"I'm so sorry," I tell him again.

"Hey—I was impressed." He grins. "I didn't know you pack such a punch—er, I mean, kick!"

"How's your throat?"

He holds my door open for me, then runs around to his side of the car.

"It still hurts a little when I swallow, but I'll be fine, Ava. It looked a lot worse than it was. I bit my tongue—that's why there was so much blood."

"Maybe you should just go home and rest tonight," I tell him. "We could do this some other time."

"Are you kidding?" Darryl says as we pull out of the parking spot, sending scraps of salt and dirt flying. "Not on your life. I've been waiting a long time for this opportunity. A little esophageal discomfort isn't going to keep me from showing you the town."

"I think I've seen pretty much all there is to see around here . . ."

"You'd be surprised," Darryl says.

We drive in silence for a while.

"Ava," he starts to say. "I know you're upset about Emily . . ."

"It's okay," I tell him. I'm not sure I want to hear about the gory details.

"I just want you to know it was a long time ago," he presses on. "Five years maybe. It wasn't long after I first came out here."

I stare at the Chocolate Mountains, trying to quell the queasy feeling.

"I was going through a rough time. My wife had died about a year before that."

My stomach lurches again. "I didn't know you were married."

"For three years," he says. "Everything happened pretty fast after she was diagnosed with ovarian cancer."

"I'm so sorry . . ." My mantra. It feels different this time, though.

"I was completely lost. I didn't know what to do with my life. When the position down here opened up, I jumped at it. I wanted to get away from all the memories up north, you know, but when I got here, it wasn't any better. This place looked as desolate as I felt."

I nod, my voice stuck in my throat.

"I was drinking when I met Emily—drinking way too much those days. It was just so nice to have someone smile at me, you know? So nice to have someone want to touch me again."

I shudder involuntarily.

"It lasted less than a week, Ava. It just didn't feel right. We had nothing to talk about. I felt emptier than ever."

I open my eyes wide to keep from crying.

"To tell you the honest truth, I was worried I'd never be able to love anyone again . . ." He looks over at me. I meet his eyes for a second, then turn my head to look out the window again, dizzy. We drive in silence until Darryl pulls the Jeep into the driveway of Shield's Date Garden.

"I thought we'd stop for a little movie before dinner," he says. "Make it a real date."

I look at the rows upon rows of date palms. "When you say date, you really mean it." My voice feels scratchy, like I haven't used it in ages.

"I always say what I mean." His eyes find mine again. I worry I won't remember how to breathe. He gets out and opens my car door.

"They have a great film here," Darryl says as I hop down to the dirt. "It's the only movie theater for miles, you know. No popcorn, but it's nice and cool inside. Don't get put off by the title—I don't mean anything by it, Ava, honestly. It's just fun, you know—a bit of local lore."

I can't imagine what he could be talking about until I notice the sign advertising the film *Romance and Sex Life of the Date.* I can feel sweat begin to form on my upper lip. I wonder if I should turn around, feign a stomachache, a heart attack. The sign, however, also touts the air conditioning and the 108 COMFORTABLE THEATER SEATS. It would be good to get out of the heat.

In the empty theater, I find myself strangely stirred by the erotic life of the date. I don't like the fact that the palms are divided into "harems," an acre of forty-eight female plants with one male "presiding"—it sounds too much like my mother's life as a bar girl—but the actual date reproductive process makes my body respond in ways I wouldn't have expected.

When the film's narrator speaks of how each female blossom must be pollinated by hand, I become acutely aware of Darryl's fingers, folded neatly on his lap. I am tempted to touch his sleeve, his arm, his wrist, but I hold myself back. *I've never tried Ecstasy before and I have no intention of ever doing so.* I have a feeling those words will haunt me the rest of my life.

After the movie, we wander over to the gift shop and taste samples of Medjool, Zahidi, Khadrawy, Halawy, and Deglet Noor dates, along with dates rolled in coconut and little date pellets dusted with oat flour. Darryl points out a package of dates stuffed with walnut pieces. The way the fruit is spread open, with the little nubbin of nut in the center, makes it look like a tray of plastic-wrapped vulvas. My pulse drops down between my legs.

"So, you mentioned dinner . . ." My voice is wavery.

"Well, I just thought we could eat dates all night."

I look at the package again and involuntarily gasp.

"Just kidding!" he grins. "I should ask, though—are you vegetarian?"

I shake my head. I've barely eaten meat—certainly not bird meat—since I've been out here, but I couldn't live without my mother's *bulgogi.*

"I mostly am, myself," he says. "But I suspend all dietary considerations for this place. Everything's dripping with lard."

"What place is it?"

"It's a little tacqueria in Mecca," he says. "My own personal Mecca de Manteca."

"Sounds good," I tell him, even though I'm hesitant to replace the taste of the dates with something else. The prickly sweetness reminds me of the Korean New Year, seeing over walls.

"Oh, it's more than good." He grins broadly. "It's ecstasy."

The tacqueria is a tiny place—a kitchen with an outdoor ordering counter and four picnic tables, all filled, on a little patio glutted with plaster statues and tubs of cactus. Christmas lights twinkle from the wrought-iron fence. The air is rich with the smell of meat and grease and onions, tempered by the powdery scent of fresh tortillas. Music, heavy on the accordion and horns, crackles out from a small speaker mounted by the roof.

"They have amazing *jamaica* here." Darryl points to a huge glass jar on the counter filled with garnet-colored liquid and ice cubes. Dark reddish things that look like tongues and sea anemones float around inside. The handle of a ladle hangs over the top of the jar.

"What in the world is that?" I ask.

"It's like a punch," he says. "It's made out of hibiscus flowers."

"Those things look more animal than vegetable," I say.

"I'll get us some," he says. "Is there something you really want to try, or do you trust me to order for you? I know what's really good here."

The menu, handwritten on a dry erase board, is all in Spanish. I recognize "taco" and "burrito," but beyond that, I'm lost. "I trust you."

"Good," he grins. "I'm glad to hear it."

"I'll go save that table," I tell him, as a couple of men get up— day laborers, probably, bandanas loose around their necks. When my route took me to Mecca, I would often see groups of men lined up along the side of the road, waiting for people to drive up and offer them work—in the fields, on a construction site, wherever under-the-table work was needed. One of them tips his cowboy hat at me as he leaves.

Darryl comes to the table with two Styrofoam cups of *jamaica*. The drink is musky and sweet, like perfume that has been on someone's body.

"That hits the spot," he says after a long gulp. "*Muy bueno.*"

A woman comes to the table with a tray of food.

"*Gracias,*" Darryl says.

"*De nada,*" she tells him. She looks at me curiously. I look away until she leaves again.

The table is covered with plates, food swimming with blobs of orange oil, sour cream everywhere. Pickled carrots and jalapeños are scattered along the edges of the entrées. I can't make sense of most of it. I pick up what appears to be a taco and take a bite. The meat, wrapped in a greasy corn tortilla, is the most tender I have ever tasted. It seems kind of like beef, but kind of not, satiny and mellow.

"What is this?" I ask.

"*Lengua,*" he says. "It's amazing, isn't it?"

"It's delicious." I take another bite. "I've never heard of it before."

"It's tongue."

I spit my mouthful of it into a napkin. "Tongue?!"

"They have tripe and sweetbreads and brains here, too, but I didn't order them."

I feel light-headed.

"Tongue is the best thing on the menu, Ava, honest. You said you trusted me, right?"

"I just wasn't expecting . . ." But I was hoping, wasn't I? Haven't I imagined his tongue—the texture, the taste of it in my mouth? *His* tongue, not a cow tongue. I feel dizzy, but I can't tell if it's from disgust or desire.

"I'm sorry, Ava," he says. "Try this—there's no meat at all, other than the lard in the beans . . ." He points to what appears to be a large shoe made out of cornmeal, filled with beans and a crumbly white cheese, sprinkled with lettuce and tomato and onions.

I take a bite from the plastic fork he holds out and close my eyes. The cornmeal is chewy and satisfying, the beans are like velvet, the cheese adds the right salty bite.

"It's a *sope*," he says. "It was my wife's favorite. There was this place in the Mission we used to go . . ." He trails off, misty.

"I'm so sorry, Darryl . . ." Those words again—they keep rising into my mouth like heartburn.

"So." He wipes his eyes. "I've told you my saddest story. You tell me yours."

I take a sip of my *jamaica* and practically choke on the piece of hibiscus that comes through the straw.

"Are you okay?"

I nod, my eyes tearing. I chew the flower bit, rubbery and sweet between my teeth.

"So, tell me. Who's broken your heart?"

I don't know where to begin. "I've broken my own heart, I guess."

"How's that?"

"I've never had a real relationship before," I tell him.

He puts his hand to his heart. "You don't strike me as someone who just fools around."

"I've never really fooled around, either . . ." The choking tears slip into real tears. I hope he won't notice the difference.

"Ava, are you okay?" He touches my hand.

I nod. The tears are streaming now.

"What is it?" he asks.

I can't answer.

"Did someone do something to you?"

He must think someone molested me when I was young. I shake my head. "My mother . . ." I start crying so hard that I almost throw up—I can feel a petal climbing up my throat.

Darryl comes around the table and puts an arm around me. I collapse into him, sobbing. We sit like this for a long time.

"Hey, do you remember that old commercial?" He fingers a pink packet in a chipped bowl on the table as I start to calm down. "'Wherever you go, Sweet 'N Low'?"

"I think so," I say, my voice trembling.

"It's like that for me, you know," he says. "Wherever I go, Ava Sing Lo."

I don't know what to say.

"I can't stop thinking about you, Ava," he whispers into my hair.

"You don't know anything about me." I start to cry again.

"But I want to," he says. "I want to know *everything* about you. I want to know your favorite color, I want to know what you looked like when you were a little girl, I want to know what kind of toothpaste you use and why you always smell like ginger and how you got that scar on your kneecap, and—"

"My mother was a prostitute," I blurt out before I realize I am going to say it.

I feel like I'm going to die, or at least explode into a million pieces, but nothing happens. I've said the words and the world didn't end. I feel exhilarated, like a ton of new oxygen has been pumped into my blood. I feel like now that I've said this, I can say anything. But I don't. Darryl wraps me in his arms and I let my lips speak to his without any words at all.

Helen stumbled down a dirt alley, holding her stomach. Bile rose fierce in her throat; she had to keep it burning there, she had to keep moving, at least another block. The night air skimmed her face like angry sweat as she rushed past a row of small tin-roofed houses, her shirt slipping off one of her shoulders.

"Are you okay?" A man's voice startled her. She stopped in her path. Before she could answer, Helen threw up—a white, clotty arc that hit his polished shoes.

"Come on," he said. "You need to lie down."

Men often said that to her, but not with the same tone of voice, not with such soft concern. Usually it was a terse command. *Lie down.* Or *Kneel, Bend over, Stand against the wall.* Like something someone would say to a dog or a naughty child. Just an hour before, Helen had been asked to squat under a table at Wild Ting and suck off five GIs, one by one, rotating between them like a windup toy beneath the cheap gum-studded particle board.

Helen threw up again, this time all over the man's pant leg. She hadn't been able to hold anything down lately. Helen figured she was pregnant; she recognized the symptoms she had seen in other pregnant bar girls—the queasiness, the deep fatigue, the darkness across the bridge of the nose—plus, her period, normally so regular, was already almost two weeks late. She had started throwing up the day Sun was killed.

"It's okay, it's okay," she could hear the man say, as he grabbed her elbow. He was pale, almost colorless, she saw as she turned her head, his hair a pelt of beige stubble, his eyes slate gray. His face was as smooth as it was white, his hands were, too. Helen cringed as he guided her through the dark walkways to a clinic, his large warm palm wrapped just beneath her bicep. She hoped no one would see her, a DMZ *kijich'on* with this ghost of a man.

The clinic was one she had never been to before, far different from the clinic where she checked in each week to be tested for an assortment of venereal diseases. A nurse put a check mark on the back of her identification card there, beneath the chart of her menstrual schedule, to show she was clean. She brought the card back to the club and put it in a cardboard box beneath the bar, where Knute kept the IDs handy. The last club owner, after the shiny suit man, was Madame Karen Carpenter Cher, an ex–bar girl from Pusan who never let her girls work when they had their period. The new owner, though—Knute, a squat American expatriate and ex-GI—just put the "bleeders" on extra blow job duty. "Their mouth ain't bleeding," he would joke to the GIs as he sent them off with their chosen orifice. When Cher was the boss, sometimes Helen stained the back of her dress with ketchup or chili sauce after her period was over, just so she could get a couple of extra days of rest, but with Knute there was no such reprieve.

The clinic the man brought Helen to was so white inside, it dazzled her eyes, made the middle of her forehead burn. She threw up again, on the man's lap this time, as he sat next to her. He stroked her hair, and she let herself be lulled beneath his long fingers. As she drifted in and out of consciousness, she could hear the man argue with the Korean women at the desk about whether or not they could treat Helen. It was a GI clinic, not some hootchy-kootchy joint you bring a date to, they said. Helen threw up another time. The man made a passionate plea, and a woman at the desk sighed and finally ushered them into the back part of the office.

Helen sat down on an examining table covered with crinkly paper, a cushy table, not like the hard wood one at the VD clinic. The man put a hand on her shoulder and lowered her down.

Another white man, dressed in mint green, came and spoke with the man, who referred to Helen as his fiancée. Helen felt a needle enter her upper arm where her princess sleeve ended; the fluid inside made her whole muscle sting. She bit her lip hard, grabbed the man's hand. He squeezed back, and she could see tears spring to his eyes. A second needle went in at her hip, where the doctor had yanked down the elastic waistband of her lilac polyester pants, her rosebud underwear. Demerol and Compazine, the doctor said to the man—one will calm her down, the other will stop the vomiting, but she'll be sleepy, so you better take her on home to rest.

The man thanked the doctor profusely, took Helen by the arm again, led her outside. She leaned against him, barely able to stand, the drugs circling woozy through her blood.

"You'll be okay now, you'll be fine," he whispered into her hair. He led her to what she supposed was his apartment and laid her down on a sofa. Before she could say a word of thanks, she fell into a dead sleep.

It was still dark when Helen woke up. She touched the blanket the man had draped over her. It was soft, like a stuffed animal splayed open. She rubbed her left hand up and down the fleecy material and tried to go back to sleep, but something felt wrong. She couldn't move her right arm. At first Helen thought it had fallen asleep, like it often did when some GI slept in her room, the weight of his head pressed against her bicep, but she didn't feel any tingles or pinpricks under her skin. Her whole arm seemed to contract itself into the spot the needle had gone in; her shoulder was drawn tense up to her ear. She cried out a little bit, a mewl of fear, but her voice felt strange. It was as if her tongue had grown while she slept, had filled up her mouth. When she called out, tentatively, "Help me, please, sir," her words sounded like Regina's, the deaf bar girl who worked at Wild Ting with her. Helen's jaw pulled itself over to one side and wouldn't go back. She screamed another garbled cry for help.

The man, soft with sleep, stumbled out to the couch. He flicked on a light and looked at Helen with alarm.

"I can't talk," she said, although the words came out without any clarity. She knew the man hadn't heard her voice before, and she was worried he would think that was how she always spoke. She gestured to her mouth and shook her head violently. Without another word, the man scooped her up and ran her back to the clinic, in his pajamas.

"Something's wrong," he said, panicky, as soon as they got through the door. "She's having some kind of seizure, her mouth is all twisted . . ."

"Does she have a history of this kind of episode, sir?" the woman at the desk, a different one, asked coolly, as she ruffled through some files.

"I don't know."

Helen shook her head.

"No," he said. "She doesn't. She was in here before, they gave her a shot, two shots. She was puking . . ."

"Is she pregnant?" the woman asked.

"No, of course not," said the man, and Helen didn't correct him.

"I'll get the doctor, sir," she said. It was a good five minutes before she came back, and during that time Helen felt like her jaw was going to crack open, to shatter apart. It felt unhinged, worse than after giving five blow jobs in a row; it felt like her lower jaw was planning on leaving the rest of her in the dust, like it was trying to break through her skin and fly away. Helen understood; she wanted to fly out of her skin herself. The first shot made her feel like she was floating for a while, but she fell asleep before she could travel very far, her friend Sun's voice warbling in the distance.

A doctor came out a couple of minutes later, right after Helen's jaw spasmed and she bit into her tongue. Blood filled her mouth, dripped over her lip. She had tasted her own blood slightly less than a year before when a GI punched her after she sneezed with him in her mouth, and her teeth clamped into his penis. A thin scar lay jagged on her top lip where her tooth had passed through. Madame Karen Carpenter Cher was in charge then and had let Helen rest until her mouth healed up, in her own room. If anything happened to a girl that couldn't be covered up with makeup under Knute's command, she was sent to the squalid Monkey House in the mountains, where they sent all the bad VD cases, until she was presentable again.

"She's having a stroke?" the woman at the desk asked the doctor.

"I'm not stroke on him!" Helen wanted to defend herself, but she couldn't get the words out. How could that woman think she would stroke the doctor at a time like this, although his zipper was within reach, and she could have if he asked.

"She's having a dystonic reaction to the medicine Dr. Salinas gave her earlier today," the doctor said to the woman, to the man who brought Helen in, to everyone but Helen. "I'm going to give her some Benadryl intravenously. We'll keep an eye on her for a while. She'll be fine."

"She's my fiancée," the man piped up. "Can I stay with her?"

"If you want." The doctor strode off to get the IV equipment. "Good luck," he said under his breath.

The nurse guided the IV needle into the back of Helen's hand; she felt herself fly out of her body with the shock of it. The Benadryl burned in, worse than the injection earlier, stinging its way down her vein, and she was sucked back into her skin. She willed herself to fall asleep as the man held her other hand, stroked the path of each vein, one by one, up to her wrist.

*   *   *

Later, back in the man's apartment, Helen dozed on and off on the couch. The man—James, he finally told her—was never far from her side, bringing her juice and tea whenever her eyes opened.

"Will you marry me?" he asked Helen as she forced some tea down her raw throat. She had not spoken one word to him yet other than her garbled cries for help.

"What you know from me?" Helen asked. "Why you want to marry this?"

"I knew the moment I saw you," said James, "when you threw up, it was just so white. The puke of an angel. I saw that, and I knew, yes-siree, that's the woman for me. Everything inside of her is pure as the driven snow. Don't find that too often round here, you know."

"You not know me." Helen shook her head. She considered asking him if he wanted a good time, giving him the price rundown, but she resisted.

"I'm flying to the air force base in Miramar, near San Diego, in less than a month—that's in California, you know—and I'd like you to come with me," James persisted, his gray eyes earnest, near tears.

You crazy boy, was all Helen could think, but then she remembered Sun's desire to go to California. *Hollywood, California,* she heard Sun's voice—Sun's Folk Village voice, not her Wild Ting voice—ring out, full of hope. Maybe Miramar was near Hollywood, California. Helen would find it for Sun, she decided. She would get out of this place alive.

Helen soon found herself attending classes at the USO Bride School, where she learned about such things as the military lifestyle, the U.S. health care system, and how to prepare American-style breakfasts and instant pudding desserts. She found herself trying not to lock eyes with the other bar girls in the class, the ones who stirred up scrambled eggs with extra care, trying not to look coarse, trying not to arouse suspicion. She found herself throwing away her *kijich'on* ID. She found herself saying "I do" in the chapel. She found herself leaving all her clothes and makeup behind at Wild Ting, never to look at Knute's ham face again. She found herself on an airplane, bound for the United States of America.

Helen couldn't believe how her heart fluttered, like wings in her chest, when she was up in the air, flying over the ocean. All around them, newlywed couples kissed and pawed at each other. Some GIs had blankets over their laps, their wives' heads moving underneath. James tentatively put his hand on Helen's knee, touched her hand as if he didn't believe she was real. She wasn't, in a way, wasn't there in the cramped seat next to him. She was out in the thin blue air, out in the pale wisps of cloud, where she always knew she would feel at home.

D arryl and I have been spending a lot of time together, but we are taking it slow—my choice, I'm afraid, not his. I love being near him, I love kissing him—the warm wet rush of it—but whenever he puts his hand on the front of my shirt, or high on my thigh, I clench like a fist. My whole body clamps down. I can't bring myself to put my own hands anywhere but his back, his face, his hair. I tell him I'm sorry again and again—I can't seem to stop myself from saying it. He's patient, but I can tell he's frustrated.

Emily is doing much better now. She came out of her coma after a couple of days. The doctors were worried about brain damage, but as soon as she woke up, she made a huge stink, demanding that someone bring one of her negligees from home; no way was she going to be caught dead in a hospital gown. After Emily started her physical therapy, Frieda showed up with the Miss Tomato tiara and sash and makeup kit; she glammed Emily up and pushed her around the hallways of the hospital; Emily waved from the chair as if she were queen of the parade. She's the same old Emily, pretty much. Her speech is a tiny bit slurred, and she seems to drag her left foot a little, but overall she's doing much better than anyone expected. I told her I've forgiven her; it seemed like the right thing to do, although part of me feels like I should have thanked her—Darryl never would have known how I really felt, *I* never would have known how I really felt, without that little chemical nudge. She says she doesn't remember why I would need to forgive her, says she doesn't remember the rave at all, and *drugs? Whatever would she be doing with drugs?* Her memory seems fine otherwise, for the most part, although she says she doesn't remember the attack. She insists she was hit by a car, but I don't know how even she could convince herself that a car would leave finger marks on her throat.

The birds are doing much better, too; the botulism seems to have run its course. We find very few dead birds now, and the pelicans that survived have all been rehabilitated and released. The out-of-state workers have gone back to their home posts. The bird hospital is eerily empty, the incinerator silent and cold. Bird organs have been shipped off to research facilities. The statistics people are firming up their calculations. The death smell is slowly fading away.

Now that I don't have to do my route as often, I find myself with more time to work on my mother's story, to fiddle around with the tapes I've been compiling. I bring my sound equipment to Darryl's house and play with it with my headphones on while he does his paperwork. It feels so easy being there with him, working side by side. It feels so easy until he reaches for me. I look at his bed, his fingers, and my mind flares, but my body can't seem to catch up.

"Ava, it's okay to feel good," he tells me, as I pull away from his hand yet again. I bite my lip to keep from crying. No one's ever said this to me before. I certainly haven't been able to say it to myself.

"You feeling good isn't going to hurt your mother."

Adrenaline shoots down my legs, a cold river.

"Think about it," he says. "She had such a rough time. You don't have to. She probably wants you to feel good, don't you think? Wouldn't she want that for you? I know I do . . ." His fingers trace the inseam of my jeans.

"I'm sorry, Darryl . . ." I can still taste his mouth—rich and dusky as cedar—inside mine. I can still taste my mother's sorrow, my own contribution to her pain. I want to chase her out of my head, but it's like she's rooted there.

"If you don't want to be here, just tell me, Ava. You don't have to humor me along."

"It's not that," I tell him. "I want to be here. You know I do. Just give me some more time, okay?"

He kisses the top of my head and walks off to the bathroom, a little hunched over. I know he is going to try to will his arousal away, maybe touch himself to relieve the pressure, and I feel so guilty, but I just can't go there with him, not yet.

I keep missing my mother's calls. She calls to tell me she saw some of the pelicans being released at Casa Cove, dozens of them being ushered out of dog carriers, unfolding their wings, taking to the sky. She calls to tell me I have been offered a job—a temporary one, a well-paying one—as a Foley person for an animation studio project in Los Angeles. She leaves the number on the answering machine. I haven't called them back yet. It makes sense to take the job—my savings are not deep enough to support me much longer—but, much to my surprise, I'm not sure I'm ready to leave here.

I finally call my mother to give her Darryl's number in case she needs to reach me in an emergency. "I'm not sleeping there or anything," I tell her. "I'm just spending more time there now."

I am prepared for her to give me a lecture, to say "*Chosim haseyo*"—"Be careful," like Kane always used to squawk at me—but she just says "He a nice man" before she hangs up. Her time with him in the bird hospital must have impressed her. I don't think I've ever heard her use the terms "nice" and "man" together before in my life. When I exhale, I feel like it's a breath I've been holding a long, long time.

James had lost his virginity to Helen their wedding night. Helen pretended to, too—she cried out like she had a hymen to break. She had a hard time acting inexperienced; she was tempted to pull out her bag of tricks, ask him if he wanted anything kinky, offer herself like clay or mud, not porcelain.

It almost annoyed Helen how grateful James was for her. When he stroked her inner arm or her neck like it was a marvel of nature, she wanted to swat his hand away. Helen was grateful for the fact that he never lasted very long—five minutes at the very most. Less than a minute the first time.

James was adamant about having a baby, so when Helen pretended like her period was late a couple of weeks after they were married, he was ecstatic. She was glad she wasn't that far along when they met—she wouldn't have too much to explain when she started showing earlier than she should have. James was more involved with the pregnancy than Helen was. If Helen had laid an egg, which she would have much rather done, James would have been the one to keep it warm.

Helen *ate* eggs, though, one after another—hard-boiled, fried, scrambled. Her husband was thrilled—a good source of protein, good Western food for the growing baby. She never told him she had heard her mother advise a pregnant neighbor to not eat eggs—they slip the spine right out of the baby's body, her mother had said, so the baby is born floppy, no backbone to support it; the baby will not live long. If the baby were born strange, maybe James wouldn't notice the color of its skin. Although she normally didn't eat bird flesh, Helen asked her husband for the money to buy duck meat—her mother had said it would fuse the baby's extremities. He was tickled by her gourmet wishes but told her it was too costly. "I'll bring you chicken," he said. "Everything tastes like chicken anyway. And it's cheap."

He came home the next day with a bag full of chicken thighs and a scrapbook, so that Helen could keep track of how many calories she ate each day, how many vitamins, and, later, so she'd have a place to paste in baby pictures and note first smile, first words. Her first impulse was to rip out the pages, but she swallowed that down and pushed the book under the bed. She felt the blank paper wait underneath her, silently taunting her when she tried to sleep, when James crawled on top of her large belly. She felt the pages daring her to write. She felt herself fill with words, new jagged English words, words she could never say to James. One day, when James was on duty, she spread the pages open like wings across her lap. She found a new place to hide the book, under the ironing board, where she knew he would never look. She let the words spill . . .

Bird fall out of nest. Baby.
Find on sidewalk, on way to commissary (milk).
No feathers, eyes purple with skin cover.
Pink yellow body to see inside. Heart stopping.
Big head, neck bent bad, little wing open.
No want to touch it. Leave there. Walk home
other way.

Sun, friend Sun, neck bent bad same way,
purple all around. Sun, where they take you?
You fly away? You go over wall?

White husband drive silver plane, make me
drink milk milk milk.
Dark baby flutter inside.

Helen knew the baby's father was black, although she wasn't sure which black man in particular. She hoped that the baby would favor her skin color, that it wouldn't be too dark. Some of the men she serviced had lighter skin than she did, freckled yellow, honey brown. One man had even been an albino, his skin chalky, his afro a frizzled, jaundiced-looking white. Maybe it was his baby. Comments from James had made it clear that he did not like black people—niggers, he called them, darkies, spades, even *ggum-doongi*. When James prayed for the baby to be healthy, Helen prayed for it to not be black.

While she was pushing the baby out, Helen went crazy. The baby got stuck, and she had to push for over an hour. Things flew out of her mouth she couldn't control. "I suck you, ten dollar," she yelled. "You put it in my asshole?" "What you want? You want good time?" She couldn't stop. A nurse tried to reassure James that women said the strangest things during labor, it wasn't her talking, it was the pain, but he sat, blanched even whiter, on a chair next to the bed, dumbfounded, his hands in his lap. He had held her hand the whole labor until she had screamed out, "I suck that big black cock? You put that big black cock in me?" and he dropped her hand like it was a pile of dog shit.

Then the baby was born black, and Helen watched James's lips press themselves into a thin blue line. She watched his hands clench and unclench. She watched the warmth of his gray eyes melt down into steel. He didn't say another word, got up, left for three days without calling. When he came back after the hospital called him to come get his wife and baby, he showed up stubble-faced, beer on his breath, his clothes rumpled. Helen held the baby wrapped so thoroughly in blankets, her face was engulfed in deep layers of cotton. Helen hoped the white cloth would reflect off the dark face, lighten the baby, but if anything, it accentuated the contrast.

James pushed the wheelchair down the hallway with such force, Helen thought her episiotomy stitches would split open, thought the baby would fly out of her arms.

"Sir, it's regulation that hospital personnel push the wheel-chair," said a young black nurse.

"Fuck off," James grunted, and ran the rest of the way. Helen closed her eyes and pulled the shrieking baby close to her chest, just starting to prickle with milk, as they hurtled their way toward the bright automatic doors.

I stop by the trailer to grab some more tapes when an unfamiliar car—a gold Mercury Zephyr, early eighties, probably, spotted with Bondo, pulls up. My mother gets out, along with another woman—Anchee, the woman from Luk's Market. She has a bruise around her left eye. Both of them look at me slightly perturbed.

"We look all over for you!" says my mother. "We drive around, look at bird hospital, look at restaurant, look at here, you not anywhere!"

"Three time we come round here!" Anchee says. I can't help but smile, thinking of the Cahuilla myth.

"I'm sorry—I was at Darryl's house."

"We not know where that is!" Anchee says. Her hand flutters up to her bruise.

I look in the car. It is stuffed to the gills with clothes and pots and pans and houseplants and two birdcages—Yukam's, and one with what looks like a small robin inside.

"Don't you touch those birds!" my mother says.

"No you touch the birds," Anchee echoes. "Your mother tell me what you do. Shame in you!"

Shame in me, yes, I think to myself. So much shame. Too much shame. So much I can't even bear to think about it.

"Omma, it looks like you're moving in."

She and Anchee nod. "Good for work on egg," says my mother. "Palm Springs nearby, many craft fair, many people want to buy fancy egg."

I open the car door and start to unload some of her stuff, stunned.

"What about the apartment in San Diego?"

"I move out," she says. "I don't wanna stay in broken egg place."

"What did you do with all the furniture?"

"I call someone, they take it away," she shrugs. "They give me a few dollar for it."

"What about your car?" I ask my mother.

"I sell it," she says.

"For how much?"

"Your mother get seven hundred dollar," Anchee says proudly.

"Omma," I groan. "You could have gotten three times that much!"

My mother shrugs.

"Don't you think you should have warned me about all this first? What if there wasn't any space in the trailer?"

"You say you at Darryl house . . ." She has a hard time with the syllables of his name—it sounds like a gurgle in her mouth.

"I'm not sleeping there . . ." I don't know what else to say. I turn to Anchee. "It was nice of you to drive her out."

"Anchee stay, too," my mother says.

"Here?"

"Me and you sleep in bed," she says. "Anchee sleep in couch. Or me and Anchee sleep in bed, you sleep in couch. Or just me sleep in bed, Anchee sleep in couch, you sleep in Darryl house."

"Omma!" I'm shocked she would even suggest this. Every time she's noticed me even look at a man before, she's jumped down my throat.

"He don't care if you a black girl." I can't tell if this is a statement or a question.

"No, of course not," I tell her, although I've wondered if that's what initially attracted him to me—a whole different kind of skin to touch. I'd like to think it was more than that, that some mysterious force brought us together, but I don't really know.

"People always surprise you come out of me. When you little girl, sometimes I pretend I a baby-sitter for you so people don't say nasty thing."

"Omma, I'm sure people didn't care as much as you thought they did. I don't know if people ever really noticed us at all."

She looks at me like I have no idea what I'm talking about, then starts to pile the contents of the car on the trailer lift.

Over the next week or so, I sleep on the couch and let my mother and Anchee take the bed. They moved all of my clothes into kitchen cabinets so that I won't have any reason to go near the birdcages in the bedroom. I go over to Darryl's house to get away, but I feel a different kind of pressure there.

"Maybe you should take Ecstasy again," he says, only half kidding, as we sit on the edge of his bed, rumpled and breathing hard after another marathon kiss. "Maybe it would help you get over this hump."

"No pun intended, right?" I lean into him. He laughs and kisses my forehead.

"I can give you a better kind of ecstasy myself, Ava. I like to think I can, at least."

I bite my lip.

"My version is a lot less dangerous than X, too," he says. "It's all natural, no side effects. There is, however, a chance that you'll find it addictive. A good chance, I hope."

I'm sure he knows this feels way more dangerous to me than any pill ever could. My mother's whole history, my whole history, weigh on me like a bag of dead birds. She's essentially given me her blessing to be here, but it's a heavy blessing, almost a burden. I don't know how I'll be able to shake it all off. I want to, more and more all the time. I want to be able to shake it all off.

Darryl scooches off the bed and kneels in front of me. I hold my breath.

"I want to help you feel good, Ava. It's driving me crazy."

"I know . . ." *Go away, Omma. I don't need you here.*

He touches the top button of my shirt. "Is this okay? Please tell me this is okay."

My mother's outline hovers inside my head. *This isn't going to hurt you,* I tell her. *I don't have to hurt like you.* Her molecules shimmer like dust. When I breathe out, some of the particles scatter. *This is a good thing, Omma. Please go away.* Her outline begins to fade. I start to feel guilty for chasing her off, but before she can gather herself together, reassert herself again in my mind, I turn to the warm real bulk of Darryl's body.

"I should warn you," I tell him, my heart at a furious boil. "I have weird nipples."

He looks amused. "Do they shoot root beer? Do they talk?"

"They're inverted. They point in." I flush. I've never told anyone about my nipples before. The only conversation I've ever had about them was when I was about eleven and my mother came into the bathroom when I was in the tub. She looked at my chest and told me no man would ever want a strange girl like me. She seemed happy about this, relieved, like I had found a way to save myself.

"They're yours," he smiles, and slips the button through its hole.

My breath catches. "I'm really scared, Darryl."

"And you think I'm not? Look at this . . ." His fingers tremble as he undoes another button.

"Just the shirt, okay?" I lie back on the bed, more stiffly than I would have liked. I think of the woman I found on the beach, her nipple lifeless between my fingers, her body rigid. I think of my mother in Kunsan, the first time she was with a man. Her body must have been stiff then, too, contracted against his foreign body, wooden with fear. I've never let myself visualize that exact moment; I skimmed over it when I wrote that part of her story. She's never given me any specific details about that night; I don't know if I could handle them.

I shouldn't be thinking about this right now. Omma, please forgive me if I'm not going to think about this right now.

Darryl kisses my lips, then parts the fabric at my breastbone and kisses there, too. My muscles loosen, turn warm and fluid as the night at the rave. I begin to feel far from dead, far, far from my mother. Wherever Darryl's mouth touches, my skin unfurls like wings.

My mother has filled up all the pages of her Book of Dead Birds. She keeps the book prominently displayed on the coffee table so that I'll see it as soon as I wake up on the couch each morning. She doesn't want me to forget all the evidence stacked against me.

I buy her a new scrapbook, one with a bright-green cover. I tell her she can use it for bird-watching, for recording all the birds, the live birds, she notices around the sea. I pick up some binoculars, a guidebook, for her at the visitor's center. People travel from all over the world to watch birds here when there's no die-off in effect; if she decides to do this, she should have no problems filling up the pages.

Anchee has been busy with her own books, keeping records of her snack sales. She stole boxes and boxes of candy from her husband's store before she left. She convinced Frieda to let her set up a little candy display by the cash register. She is at the Aloha now, arguing over Frieda's percentage.

I don't know yet what I'll do with my notebook about my mother's life, don't know if I'll ever show it to her. I still have so many questions.

My mother finishes blowing an egg. A final teardrop of albumen hangs from the shell; she sweeps it off with a rag.

"Omma," I say. "You've never told me what happened next."

"What happen next when?" She wipes her lips with the back of her hand, sets the eggshell down.

"What happened after I was born. After you left the hospital."

"Oh, that." She turns away, picks the eggshell back up, looks at it as if it is the most interesting object on earth.

"Omma, you don't have to tell me. I mean, of course I want to know, but if you don't want to . . ."

"It okay." She puts the eggshell back down.

I reach for the drum, but she doesn't start to sing. She starts to talk. She has never told me her story in her regular speaking voice before—it has always been the *pansori,* the drum, the wild fluctuations of the song. Now her voice is level, calm. I fold my hands in my lap to keep them quiet.

"He beat me up," she says. "After the hospital, he beat me up. I still bleeding from you being born and he stick his thing in me. He bite me, he hit me. He do all kinds mean thing to me."

"Oh, Omma," I say. "What did you do?"

"I run away," she tells me. "I take you and I run away. The army place so big. I not know where to go. He try and look for me. I see him run around, look for me. I run into plane."

"You crashed into a plane?" I'm confused.

"I go inside. A plane open. I go inside. He run past it, not see us there."

"What happened then?" How could I have not known about this?

"The plane go up in the air."

"With us in it?"

She nods.

"Didn't they know we were in there?"

"We in the bottom. In like a little bubble. The place where they shoot guns out."

So *that* was the first time I flew. I guess my maiden launch wasn't from a seesaw after all. "How long were we in the air?" I ask.

"Not long, but it go up and down a few time," she tells me. "It take off, go around over water, come back, come down. I think we gonna get out and then it go up in the air again. It go up and down, three time, maybe four. Up and down, up and down. I not know what gonna happen."

"Were you scared?"

"I scare they gonna find us. You scream like crazy. I think your ear hurt. My ear pop and pop. I thought they try and scare us, go up and down like that, try and make us sick."

"Maybe it was a test for a new pilot, or something."

"Who know? But I see San Diego from air. I see all kinds thing from air. Is good to see so many thing, open your mind. I see some sign, know there is place we can go."

"Did he ever find you after that?"

She shakes her head. "I one time see him, when you was 'bout five year old. I see him walk down street with yellow-hair woman and yellow-hair baby, but I not say anything."

"Omma." I touch one of her hands. Her skin is so dry. "I wish your life had been easier. I'm so sorry you've had such a hard time. I'm sorry if I've made it harder for you . . ."

She stands up, brushes herself off, and goes to get her drill. Through the open bedroom door, I can see Yukam and the baby robin stir as she walks by.

Anchee comes through the door. The way she and my mother look at each other makes me catch my breath. I wonder if they are lovers, if they are helping each other find their own pleasure, the way Darryl has been helping me. I kind of hope so, although I doubt it. I have a feeling my mother wouldn't care if no one ever touched her again. She and Anchee are probably just glad to have found a home together, to have escaped. Either way, this trailer doesn't feel like mine anymore.

*   *   *

Before I give myself a chance to chicken out, I call the Foley people to find out if the job is still available. The one they originally called me for has been filled, but my timing is good—another temporary position just opened up. I tell them I'll take it. It's just for a few months, and I can definitely use the money. I'm sure my mother will appreciate it, too—it will be a while before she has enough eggs to hit the craft fair circuit again, and Anchee's candy money, while helpful, is not going to amount to a whole lot. Plus, I enjoy Foley work—crushing potato chip bags into a microphone to simulate feet walking across gravel, waving my hand around in a bucket of water in time with the character's movements in the tub, coming up with new ways to create everyday sounds.

Darryl promises he'll come visit me in L.A., and I'll try to spend some weekends back here if I don't have too much work. Where I'll stay when I visit, where I'll stay when the job's over, I'm not sure. We'll see how it goes. The job should be done just as the Date Festival opens in Indio. Darryl and I have plans to meet there. I can already feel us going over the top of the Ferris wheel, our feet dangling in thin air, the bench lightly swaying back and forth, dizzy as the rush of flight. I think about the walnut-stuffed dates that will be waiting for us when we reach the ground, and I feel even dizzier.

As I pull my clothes from the kitchen cabinets, a small piece of paper flutters out from between some socks. It's the poem, the *kisaeng* poem my mother tucked into my drum before I left San Diego. The last two lines haunt me:

Stay just as far away as you can;
time will keep or lead you back.

I never thought there would be anything to keep me here, never thought it would be so hard to leave this place. I feel like I need to do something, something special, to mark my time here, to bring some sort of closure to the rescue effort.

When I was at SDSU, a portion of the AIDS quilt came to campus. People signed up to read names of AIDS victims over a microphone that projected out onto the quad. Each person read for five minutes. I sat in the grass, too shy to get up and read. I let the names wash over me like ghosts, felt waves of sadness at each syllable, each name that meant more than itself, that encompassed a whole person, a whole history, a past of favorite foods, deepest fears, a past of music and pain and love, each name meaning so much more than the words suggested. There were so many names, and I tried to honor each one I heard, let it travel through me, leave its mark.

It all suddenly makes sense. For the first time in a long time, maybe the first time ever, everything finally seems to make sense. I start working on my tapes in earnest.

The Aloha is dim; the only light comes from the inflatable hula girl, a soft glow in her belly. The self-defense class is assembled; everyone is here—Emily and Frieda, the bridge ladies, Lonnie, Rayanne with her pink poodle hair piled high. Everyone is wearing a traditional white Do-Bok. We stand in a circle, ready.

The door opens. A man walks in, wearing a self-defense suit, padding everywhere, a huge puffy helmet. We charge at him. He tosses Emily across the room, throws the bridge ladies over the counter all in one swoop. Rayanne pummels him with her dainty fists. He picks her up and hurls her through the window. Lonnie kicks him with the side of her stocky leg; he grabs her calf and pile-drives her headfirst into the floor. Frieda and I stand together, ready. He reaches for us. I know the world is about to go black, but the door opens again and the room is flooded with light. My mother stands in the doorway, holding her bow and arrow. She lets an arrow fly. Frieda and I jump back. The arrow pierces the chest of the man's self-defense suit. Blood gushes from it like a geyser. She must've hit him in the heart. He crashes to the ground.

When we're sure it's safe, we remove the man's helmet. It's not a man at all, it turns out, but a bird, a huge bird. An albatross, its head turned to the side, its beak open. "It not bother you anymore," my mother says. A chain falls from my neck. I float up to the ceiling, suddenly weightless. Free.

I stand at the end of the pier at North Beach, where I first saw all the dying pelicans. Darryl and Frieda and Ray and Jeniece and Emily and Anchee and my mother all cluster around me. We each hold a sheet of paper, different lines highlighted on each one. My drum is strapped around my neck. My hands are ready. I give my mother the signal and she turns on the tape player. The tape I have put together, the one full of birdsong and bird silence, whirs into the air.

I hold the piece of paper out in front of me, the list of bird die-off victims Fish and Wildlife has compiled. I begin to read, out loud, with all my voice, with all the feeling I can muster. "Snowy egret, two hundred seventy-one, cattle egret, fifty-five, unidentified egrets, two hundred eighty-seven, green heron, five, black-crowned night heron, one hundred sixty-nine." I punctuate each bird name, all the bird names to come, with a drumbeat.

Darryl's voice buckles around the names, "White-faced ibis, seven, fulvous whistling duck, one, brant, one, green-winged teal, fifty-three, mallard, five."

I fiddle around on the drum until Frieda begins: "Northern pintail, twenty-seven, gadwall, seven, canvasback, two, redhead duck, twelve, lesser scaup, five."

Ray takes over: "Common merganser, two, red-breasted merganser, five, ruddy duck, twenty-seven, unidentified ducks, thirty-seven, osprey, two."

Jeniece is next: "Sora rail, one, American coot, one hundred and four, black-bellied plover, four, semipalmated plover—did I say that right?—eight, killdeer, one."

Emily clears her throat, tosses her hair, and says in her best Miss Tomato voice, "Black-necked stilt, one hundred twenty-five,

American avocet, one hundred and seven, greater yellowlegs, one, lesser yellowlegs, six, willet, thirty-one."

"Why'd you give me yellowlegs, Ava?" she asks. "Are you saying something about my legs? Are you saying something about my gimpy leg?"

"No one's saying anything about your legs, Emily," Frieda says.

"No offense or anything, Jeniece," Emily says.

Jeniece rolls her eyes.

I turn to my mother. "Go ahead, Omma."

She stumbles over the words but stays remarkably calm: "Spotted sandpiper, one, whimbrel, ten, long-billed curlew, six, marbled godwit, eleven, ruddy turnstone, one."

When it's Anchee's turn, she shakes her head. "You do it," she tells me. "I not know how to say these name."

I let the words rise from the page: "Western sandpiper, one hundred ninety, dowitcher, seventy-three, sanderling, four, Wilson's phalarope, two, unidentified phalarope, nine."

Darryl touches my elbow, then reads, "Unidentified shorebird, sixty, Bonaparte's gull, twenty-three, ring-billed gull, six hundred fourteen, California gull, twenty-five, yellow-footed gull, three."

"Herring gull, eighty-six," Frieda continues, "unidentified gull, twenty-seven, gull-billed tern, one, Caspian tern, thirty-two, Forster's tern, eight."

Ray takes over. "Unidentified tern, eighteen, black skimmer, eighteen, American crow, one, belted kingfisher, one."

I tap a faster rhythm onto my drum.

We all read together: "Brown pelicans, eleven hundred twenty-nine, white pelicans, eight thousand five hundred thirty-eight."

I lift my hands off the drum, let the resulting silence fill the air. The tape is still whirring, offering a smattering of coos, the whoosh of the airboat. We take a collective breath, then send the names of the two women who were murdered echoing over the hills.

* * *

I am glad I can picture most of the birds we named. A few months ago, all I could identify was a crow, a sparrow, humming-bird, blue jay—common birds any child can name. Now I feel the dignity of all 14,131 lost birds, the dignity of the two lost women, pass through me like the breeze behind a hawk's tail feathers. I feel my own heartbeat trail after them.

I take a long look at the water, the water that stretches out before us, blue for once, not affected by any algae tides. I suddenly love each wrinkle, each shimmer of it. I love the mountains that rise up on each side, the Chocolate, the Santa Rosa, the Orocopia, the Superstition Hills. I love the pale-green birdshit that plasters the barnacles by my feet, the birds that circle overhead, out of danger for now. I love the people who surround me, these broken, beautiful people . . .

"You should have seen this place in its heyday," says Frieda. "All the movie stars came here—Frank Sinatra, Doris Day, all the biggies. The water was so full of people, you could barely move sometimes. There were always parties on the beach, water-skiing competitions, boat races, fishing derbies, you name it. It was spec-tacular. We thought it would last forever."

"We're going to try to save it," Darryl tells her. "It may come back."

"It would be a miracle," says Ray.

"That would be so cool if the stars came here again," says Emily. "Can't you see it, Frieda? Tom Cruise walking into the Aloha?" She tosses her hair as if he's going to show up any moment.

Darryl squeezes my hand.

"Maybe I skin-dive here," my mother says.

"Gross!" yells Emily.

"If the water get cleaner," my mother tells her. "No more fish floating around."

"Good luck," Ray says under his breath.

"You skin-dive?" Frieda asks.

My mother nods. "Women in my family dive. That what they do."

Frieda turns to me. "Do you skin-dive, Ava?"

I shake my head, surprised by the pang I feel.

I'm not the only one to end the tradition. I've read that women divers are becoming a dying breed on Cheju-do, that fish farms are setting up shop, sending their wastewater into the diving areas. The water is becoming so polluted there that the rocks change color. Now the normally abundant sea urchins yield less than a teaspoon of bright-orange meat each. Abalone are getting harder and harder to find. People are concerned about it, I've read. Maybe things will change if enough voices are raised.

"Did you hear?" Frieda pulls me aside. "They have some guy in custody. I'm supposed to take Emily in to ID him. She says she doesn't remember anything, but maybe if she sees him . . ."

I look over at Emily rolling around some barnacles with the toe of her sandal. She looks a lot shorter, more vulnerable, almost childlike, without high heels on.

"You'll have to keep me posted."

Frieda gives me a hug. "We're gonna miss you, Miss Ava Sing Lo."

I breathe in the scent of bacon from her hair. My mother is watching us, watching Frieda crush me to her body in a way she herself has never done. She blinks a few times before she turns her head; Jeniece is there, ready to catch her attention. I hear her ask my mother if she'd teach her how to swim.

When I emerge from Frieda's embrace, Darryl is waiting.

"This was perfect," he says.

I reach for his hand. The warmth of his skin travels all the way up my arm.

"It was the right thing to do," I tell him, and it was. The exact right thing. I lean my forehead into Darryl's and close my eyes. The desire to create this memorial, this new sensation of desire, a sensation I'm just learning to heed, was sharp as my palm against my drum. Insistent as the drum of my heart. Keen as the pull that first brought me to this parking lot, reeling me in like gravity, telling me that after all my circling, it's time to create my own human world.

Acknowledgments

I could fill a whole book of live birds with my gratitude.

Thanks to the Money for Women/Barbara Deming Memorial Fund for supporting me and the novel in its very early stages.

Thanks to my mentors and workshop leaders at Antioch who challenged and encouraged me as this novel was finding its form—Karen Bender, Leonard Chang, Jill Ciment, Tara Ison, Jim Krusoe, Darrell Spencer, and the magical Alma Luz Villanueva, with worshipful bowing to Diane Lefer who guided me through a radical revisioning of the book. All of my friends at Antioch were equally important to the process—thanks to each and every one of you, with special gratitude to Laraine Herring, Peggy Hong, and Sefi Ransome-Kuti; your collective talent and support amaze and sustain me. Eloise Klein Healy was such sublime mother hen for the program; I was so fortunate to have been under her wing.

Thanks to the family I was lucky enough to be born into—my parents, Arlene and Buzz Brandeis, for being my steadfast champions, my sister Elizabeth Brandeis for being my partner in crime, plus Jon and Magdalene Brandeis, Sue Ball, Craig Morrison, Mollie Morrison-Brandeis, Mimi Perretz, the Perretz-Gonzales', and all the rest of the famn damily for rooting me to this earth. Thanks to the family I was lucky enough to marry into—Patricia O'Donnell, Dick McGunigle, Sharon McGunigle, Heather McGunigle, Maggie McGunigle, Tim Ormsby, Eula Palmer, Jack Cotter, Diane and Paul

Reardon, and all the rest of my *Makheteyneste.* I'm so blessed to be part of your clan.

I can't thank my husband, Matt McGunigle, enough. This book would not exist without his belief in me. Thanks, too, to my kids, Arin and Hannah, for being the loudest members of my cheering section. I love you all so much.

Thanks to all my friends, on and off line, for your support, with special hugs to Kate Anger, Denise and Dave Brown, Jennifer Calkins, Lucia Dick, Chris Fullerton, Christian Harder, Jianda Johnson, Vicki Kelley, Donna Kennedy (Miss Salton Sea, herself!), Catherine Kineavy, Judy Kronenfeld, Kristin Kucia-Stauder, Caroline Leavitt, Kris Lovekin, Kathryn Morton, Bernadette Murphy, Cati Porter, Sakada, Sue William Silverman, Jacque Smillie, Rob Stauder, Susan Straight, Katherine Thomerson, Greg Walloch, Valerie Carlene, Susan Ito, Keta Hodgson, Linda Rigel, Lakin Khan, Greg Hyduke, Mary Sharratt, Alex Lang, Liz Newman, all my friends and beloved professors from the Johnston Center at the University of Redlands, the folks at Readerville, all writer-mamas and everyone at MYWG.

Thanks to Sonja Johnson for participating in my first dead bird ritual when we were in first grade. Thanks to the strep germs that gave me fever dreams that changed the course of the novel. Thanks to the dead crow that appeared on my patio just when I was ready to throw the story away.

Thanks to folks who gave me the lowdown about the Salton Sea situation—Norm Niver of the Salton Sea Citizens Advisory Panel, Jake Vasquez of the Salton Sea National Wildlife Refuge, and Linda York of the Coachella Valley Wild Bird Center. Your first-hand perspective was invaluable. Thanks to the documentary *The Women Outside* by J.T. Takagi and Hye Jung Park for first alerting me to the plight of women on U.S. military bases in Korea; thanks to Katharine Moon's book *Sex Among Allies* for deepening my understanding.

Thanks to the great people at James Levine Communications, especially my agent, Arielle Eckstut, for being such a marvelous force of nature (as well as a supreme mensch!). Thanks to Terry Karten and Andrew Proctor at HarperCollins for all of your wisdom and guidance and enthusiasm; I can't believe my good fortune in getting to work with you. Thanks to my posse at Harper-SanFrancisco and their continuing beneficence—Renee Sedliar and Calla Devlin, you are goddesses.

I am deeply, deeply, grateful to everyone associated with the Bellwether Prize. Barbara Kingsolver, Toni Morrison, and Maxine Hong Kingston have all been longtime idols for me, models for how to serve as a writer in the real world, how to balance art and social responsibility. To be able to acknowledge them here makes me weak in the knees. Thanks to all of you for your generosity in your work and in your life. I am humbled to have been given this incredible honor.

Kamsahamnida.